Lies They Tell Her

APPLEMAN'S GAP
BOOK ONE

KELLY UTT

2024 Standards of Starlight Paperback Edition

www.standardsofstarlight.com

ISBN: 978-1-952893-27-8

Cover art by Elizabeth Mackey

A Note on Setting

While many of the locations in this book are true to life, some details of the setting have been changed.

Appleman's Gap is a fictional town, set about an hour east of Nashville, Tennessee on the edge of the Cumberland Plateau. I envision it much like the mountainous region of the Appalachians in East Tennessee, but placed closer to Nashville. It's a small town along a winding river that empties into a picturesque lake with a bustling marina. Apple orchards line the hillsides and a railroad skirts the river bank.

Nashville, of course, is a real town, the bustling, creative capital of the U.S. state of Tennessee. Our characters in the Appleman's Gap series often go to Nashville since the fictional town is considered to be within the Nashville metro area. Like the real-life Nashville metro area, Appleman's Gap is experiencing rapid growth with new residents moving in and new construction happening everywhere.

Lies They Tell Her is a work of fiction. Any references to historical events, real people, or real places are used fictitiously. Other names, characters, places, and events are products of my imagination, and any resemblance to actual events or places or persons, living or dead, is entirely coincidental.

Thanks for reading,
Kelly Utt

PART ONE

Taken by Surprise

One

Hillside Parkway
Appleman's Gap, Tennessee

The Day After Thanksgiving
6:23pm

"9-1-1, WHAT'S YOUR EMERGENCY?"

Laurel Dane's breath caught as she pressed her ear awkwardly against the mobile phone. "Oh, thank God, you answered," she breathed. "You're there?"

The man's voice on the other end of the line was cool and smooth. "Yes, ma'am. Officer Cedric Martin here, Appleman's Gap P.D. Do you have an emergency?"

Laurel wriggled, shopping bags and wrapping paper crinkling around her. She had to muffle the sound of the dispatcher's voice. "Shh," she pleaded. "Talk quietly. He'll hear you."

"Who will hear me, ma'am?" Cedric asked, as quietly as he could. "Who is *he*?"

Laurel's hands were bound tightly at the wrists and her feet were tied at the ankles. There had been a gag in her mouth, too, but she'd managed to use the muscles in her jaws to slowly work it up and out. The dirty cloth still clung to one side of her lips, secured by twine that had been ripped from the Christmas tree on the roof of her car. Finally, after much effort, her mouth was free enough to speak.

The gag smelled of an unidentifiable chemical. Like motor oil. Although, not as sweet. The odor wasn't familiar to Laurel, but it was certainly noxious. She feared that whatever it was might cause her to lose consciousness. She did her best to breathe fresher air, from the opposite direction. There was precious little space around her.

Some Black Friday this was turning out to be.

"Ma'am, are you still on the line?"

"I'm here," she replied in a hushed tone. A single tear ran down her cheek, its wetness sticking in the cold. She was supposed to be catching criminals, not falling victim to them.

It had taken what felt like forever to dig the phone out from a shopping bag, remove the packaging, power it on, and place the call. Every step in the process had felt excruciatingly difficult. Every little noise she made had been a dangerous liability.

"Where are you?" Officer Martin asked.

"I don't know," Laurel replied. "I was at the holiday market, the open air space with the high ceilings and string lights."

"In Appleman's Gap?"

She nodded, her head bumping against something. Moving around in the cramped compartment was hard to do. "Yes. We ate lunch nearby and were doing some shopping," she explained. She spoke softly, in fits and starts. "I was at the east side of the property when he grabbed me. There must have been something on the gag because I think I was unconscious. Chloroform, maybe."

"Are you still at the market now?" the officer asked. His voice became muffled as he turned away to give instructions to someone else.

"No," Laurel said. "Not anymore. My friend Sarah went back inside because she had forgotten her scarf. That's when he got me."

Officer Martin mumbled something additional in the background. Laurel wondered what he was saying, but didn't have the mental bandwidth to try to figure it out. All of her energy was spent making sure the man who had abducted her didn't realize she was talking on a phone. That was step one in getting away.

"Are you calling from a mobile phone?"

"Yes, but he doesn't know I have it," Laurel replied. "He took my phone. Luckily, though, I had just bought a new one for my mom. It was in one of the shopping bags. I dug it out and powered it on. That's what I'm calling from now."

"Smart move," Officer Martin said. "You're doing great. I need you to stay on the line with me, okay?"

"Okay," Laurel said, another tear making its way down her face.

She debated whether to tell him that she was an F.B.I. agent, in town to visit family for the Thanksgiving holiday. She should have known better than to let herself be taken.

How embarrassing.

Laurel was freezing, her breath visible in the cold November air. She hoped she could get warm soon. It had snowed earlier in the day, and a layer of crunchy ice had formed on top. Temperatures were in the thirties and forecast to drop even further overnight.

Snow was sparse in Middle Tennessee at any time of year. The fact that it had made an appearance on this long holiday weekend was certainly special. Laurel had been delighted to see the wintry precipitation when it had arrived. The market had been alight with sights, sounds, and smells of happiness and holiday cheer. But that was before. Now, the snowscape felt foreign and cruel.

"Can you tell me your name?"

Laurel nodded, again bumping her head. She grimaced. "Yes. Laurel Dane."

"Good, Laurel. I'm going to help you, okay?"

"Please do, Officer," she replied, more tears surfacing. She bit them back, choosing instead to focus on relaying the facts. "It sounds like we're on a highway. I can hear traffic around us. I'm in the trunk of my own car. It's a late model Honda Accord. The Sport-L Hybrid model in red. Matte black alloy wheels. There is—or at least, there *was*—a Christmas tree tied to the roof."

"Good. That's helpful. What else?"

"The man who grabbed me was Caucasian. Just under six feet tall. He was well dressed, wearing a long overcoat and one of those English hats ... Flat caps, I believe they're called. He was clean and well groomed. Mid-thirties. Very short hair. Strong features. He blended into the crowd. Nothing about him seemed unusual until he approached me."

She wondered how long it would take for the dispatcher to search her name and learn her connection to the Bureau. Ol' Jimmy Paulson, her Special Agent in Charge back in D.C., would be none too pleased to find out that one of his agents had fallen victim to some petty criminal while on leave. Laurel could already imagine the talking-to she would receive when this was all over.

First, she had to break free.

"I understand," the officer said. "Can you tell me where you are now?"

Officer Martin was calm and patient. He had been trained for this, and it showed. He was handling the situation like a pro. There was a lot at stake, though. More than the officer even knew. His assistance would soon be critical to saving more than one innocent life.

"I told you, I don't know where I am," Laurel said. She was growing frustrated. "I was at the holiday market, but I think the guy knocked me out. I don't remember him binding my hands and feet. I can't be sure how long I've been in here." Despite the circumstances, she was maintaining her composure. She knew how to keep a level head under pressure. "There's a release lever in the trunk. It's not working, though. He must have disabled it somehow."

"It's okay," Cedric replied. "Let's start at the beginning. What happened at the market?"

A booming voice sounded suddenly. "Don't be gettin' any ideas back there! You hear me?" a man bellowed. "If you're awake, you better stay still and shut your whore mouth. Or else."

Laurel's body went stiff as a board, which was remarkable given how twisted it was in the tight space. She remained silent, knowing better than to speak. She had to play her cards carefully.

For someone who looked as polished as this man had, he

sure sounded gruff now. She couldn't understand the vitriol he had for her. What had she done to anger him? She had been minding her business, shopping like everyone else. Why her?

"What was that?" Officer Martin asked.

"Shh," Laurel whispered through gritted teeth. "Quiet!"

"Is it him? Tell me what's happening," the officer pleaded. "We need to know so we can help, Laurel."

Maybe it was because Laurel had let the strange man stand too close when he'd approached her in the market. Or maybe, it was because she'd held eye contact too long during their brief conversation, encouraging him to pursue her and the hope of something more. Just maybe, it was because she hadn't smacked him square across the face when he'd groped at the rise of her inner thigh. In hindsight, shouting for him to stop probably hadn't been enough of a reaction. He had grabbed her in plain sight.

"Are you tracking my location?" she asked. "Can you triangulate the signal?"

"We're working on that," the officer said. "Stay with me, okay?"

She nodded, having finally learned how to avoid hitting her head when doing so. "Okay. Maybe I can knock out a tail light. That could draw attention."

"Good idea," Cedric replied.

Yeah, it was a good idea, but Laurel couldn't help but feel like it wasn't good enough. She felt like her training had failed her. Or more like she had failed the F.B.I. Not to mention, herself.

All that time learning at Quantico and working in the field, only to be snatched like a clueless civilian. She told herself to remain calm. Yet it seemed impossible to push the feelings of shame away. They pressed against her, like the icy hands of a winter ghost.

Laurel sobbed now, though she held as much of the sound inside as she could. Turning her head, she pressed one arm against her mouth to squelch the noise. She cried for what felt like an eternity as the cold and the chemical smell moved deeper into her lungs. She couldn't help herself. She had been so strong, for so long. And being back in Appleman's Gap was bringing the painful memories to the surface.

"Laurel?" Officer Martin asked.

"He'll hear me if I talk," she breathed.

"I know, Laurel. I realize this is scary," he replied. "But you sound like you can handle it. I need you to tell me more so that my officers can find you and make sure you're safe. Now, whisper, but tell me. What happened at the market? Who is the man?"

For a moment, she didn't answer.

"Laurel?"

"I'm here," she managed. "I don't know who the man is, but I think he heard me and I'm afraid of what he might do."

The words tasted bitter coming out.

"I understand," Officer Martin said. "I'll stay on the line with you as long as it takes."

Bolstered by the officer's encouragement, Laurel took a deep breath as she felt around for a way to disable a tail light. Her hands were going numb from being bound, but she pushed through the discomfort.

"Cornelius Dane would be having a conniption fit, if he could see me now," she mumbled to herself.

There was a scratching sound as Officer Martin moved

the phone closer to his mouth. "Did you just say ... Cornelius Dane? As in the late *Chief* Cornelius Dane?"

Laurel hadn't meant to say her dad's name out loud. *Too late.* The cat was out of the bag. She sighed heavily. "That's the one. He was my dad."

"I'm sorry for your loss," the officer said. "Chief Dane was a good man. It hasn't been the same around here since he's been gone."

"Thanks," she squeaked out. She wanted to ask how well he knew her dad, but this wasn't the time.

"Let's get you to safety, okay? I owe it to your dad. Are you close to the holiday market now?" he asked.

"I don't think so," Laurel replied.

"Are you still in Appleman's Gap?"

"I honestly don't know. He's driving like a madman."

Just then, the man hit the brakes, slamming Laurel against the back seat. Her muscles tensed even tighter. She waited nervously to see if he had heard her. She knew that nothing good could happen if he found out she had dialed 9-1-1. She didn't have her service weapon on her, and she couldn't immediately come up with a plan to overpower the man, given her bindings.

"I think he's stopping," she whispered into the phone. "Please, you have to help us. I'll never forgive myself if—"

"Us? Who's with you?"

Officer Martin spoke to someone in the background again, his voice muffled.

Laurel wanted the car to stop. Sarah's infant son was in the backseat. The boy could make a sound and set the man off. Perhaps he wasn't yet aware of the child's presence.

"My friend's dog, Bear," she explained reluctantly. Saying

the words somehow made what was happening more real. More terrifying. "And Jasper, her infant son. He's buckled into his car seat. I think he's still sleeping. He's quiet, anyway."

"There's a baby in the car?" Cedric asked, his voice rising. Gone was the cool, calm demeanor from earlier.

"That's right," Laurel replied.

"Standby," the officer said, then covered the receiver on the phone as he shouted something in the background.

It seemed like forever that he was gone. Each second that ticked by felt like an eternity. Laurel expected the man to fling the door to the trunk open at any moment. Or worse, to put his hands on the baby. The car was stopped, she could tell that much for sure. But she couldn't tell if the man had exited the vehicle or if he had simply parked somewhere. Perhaps at a traffic light. Everything was disorienting from her vantage point.

Come on. Come on, she thought, hoping Officer Martin would return with some shred of good news. Maybe knowing her dad would make him work harder for her.

A car door slammed, the sound and the impact startling the baby. Little Jasper screamed and Laurel's blood ran cold.

"He's coming. He woke the baby," Laurel breathed into the phone.

Cedric heard her, and he removed whatever it was that had been muting the phone. "Agent Dane," he said solemnly, "we pulled your file. We know you're with the Bureau, which is why I'm going to tell it to you straight."

"Okay," she replied, hurriedly. "Do it fast. We're running out of time."

"There's been a rash of kidnappings all over town.

Carjackings with babies in carseats. We don't know much yet, but they seem to be targeting busy places like gas stations, shopping centers, that sort of thing. Places where the baby is left inside a vehicle unattended for a few minutes while someone is loading, unloading, or gassing up."

"Oh, my God," Laurel breathed.

"That isn't all," he continued. "Sometimes, they take the mothers, too, and sometimes ... they dump the bodies. We have a handful of missing persons and two confirmed deaths. We've managed to keep it from the media so far, but it won't be long before word gets out."

Laurel shook her head, as if the motion could make all of this go away. "It's like ..." she began. "Like before. Like what Dad was investigating ..."

Words failed. The realizations were coming too hard, too fast. Sheer terror gripped Laurel.

Officer Martin sighed as baby Jasper screamed louder. His tone was stern. "Do *everything* you can to get yourself and that baby out of there, Agent Dane. Your lives almost certainly depend on it."

Before Laurel could respond, the lid to the trunk was ripped open. The silhouette of the man came closer, his quick movements too fast for her eyes that were still adjusting to the light.

"Get out!" he shouted. "You're done."

The man yanked Laurel by her long brown hair, up and partially out of the small compartment. The mobile phone landed on the floor of the trunk with a soft thud. She steeled herself, determined to make the most of the moment and provide Officer Martin whatever clues she could. Straining against the man's effort, she wedged her feet at the front of the trunk, slowing his progress.

"I can see the lights of downtown," she said loudly and clearly as baby Jasper continued to cry from the backseat. He wailed as if his life depended on it. "The top of the court-house is visible in the distance. It looks like we're northeast of there. Maybe two miles away, as the crow flies."

"Shut it!" the man said as he continued to tug on her. Then he reared back, and smacked her hard across the face.

Pain shot through Laurel's jaw and cheekbone, but she opened her eyes against it. She kept watching, kept searching for clues. "Oh!" she exclaimed defiantly, talking loudly in the direction of the mobile phone. "A plane just flew overhead. Blue and orange. Must be Southwest. It's heading in for a landing, west of us. Probably to BNA, the international airport in Nashville—"

The man reached in and grabbed the phone, then threw it to the ground and stomped it to pieces. "Enough," he growled.

Despite her attempts to brace against the man and make his job difficult, he successfully hoisted her out of the trunk. She landed on the concrete hard. Jasper wailed.

"Leave the baby," Laurel pleaded. "Take the car. You can have it. Just leave the baby."

The man grunted as he walked around the side of the car and opened a door to the backseat. Laurel held her breath, hopeful that he would remove the baby's car seat and leave the infant with her. Bear immediately jumped out and took off, clearly spooked by what was happening.

Aww, Bear, she thought as she watched her best friend's dog disappear behind an industrial building in the distance.

He was a family pet who probably wouldn't last long on the streets. It was a sad sight, but nothing like what she was about to witness if this man took the baby.

"It'll be better for you if you leave the baby," Laurel tried. "I'll say that you didn't know he was in the car. You'll get off easy. Or maybe, you won't even get caught."

He grunted again, turning toward Laurel and narrowing his eyes. For a moment, she wondered if he had a weapon and whether he intended to use it on her. She was defenseless. She wouldn't have been able to stop him. Her life could end, right here and now.

Finally, he slammed the door of the car, baby Jasper still inside.

"No!" Laurel said as the man walked around to the trunk and slammed it, too.

"Don't do it," she pleaded. "He's just an innocent baby … Take me instead!"

The man scoffed, appraising her as she struggled on the ground. He kicked his head back and let out a sinister laugh. "Say nighty-night, mama. He's my baby now."

Then he returned to the driver's seat and sped away, tail lights disappearing into the night.

IN LITTLE MORE THAN AN HOUR, Laurel was sitting in a sparsely decorated room at the Appleman's Gap Police Department, drinking a cup of bad coffee. She wasn't even a coffee drinker, but she had taken it when the nice receptionist asked. It was likely going to be a long night. She figured the extra caffeine wouldn't hurt.

Two patrol cars and an ambulance had found her in record time. She was impressed, if she did say so herself. Her dad would have been proud of his team. Not too shabby for a small Tennessee town. Her friends back in D.C. probably wouldn't believe it, if she told them.

Of course, the EMTs had wanted to take her to the hospital to get checked out, but she declined. She had other matters on her mind that took priority, namely finding baby Jasper. Not to mention, Laurel wanted to be the one who broke the news to Sarah. It would be one of the most gut-wrenching conversations of her life, but she knew that her friend deserved to hear it directly from her rather than some random officer who didn't have a personal interest in what was happening.

Laurel used her fingertips to carefully dab at the bruises on her face. She'd given them a quick look in the bathroom mirror a few minutes prior, but the pain was beginning to develop an edge to it. Her back was sore too, along with an all-over ache she couldn't even identify, let alone fully explain. Maybe it was from being thrown around and twisted up in the trunk. Or maybe it was from the emotional trauma, which had surely led to holding her body tense as she braced for the worst.

"Agent Dane, can I get you anything?" the receptionist asked, sticking his head in the door cautiously. "More coffee?" He was a clean-cut young man who looked every bit the part of a cop, but he seemed too timid to survive out on the streets. Maybe that's why he was on desk duty.

"I'm good on coffee, thank you. Some pain killers would be great, though," she replied. "Have any?"

"Of course. Be right back, ma'am."

Thanks to her dad's reputation, everyone here was treating her like local royalty.

Maybe she was royalty. Laurel had grown up in this town. In this station.

If she closed her eyes, she could almost see the child version of herself sitting in her dad's office down the hall, working studiously with crayons and a glossy coloring book while she waited on him to wrap up what he was doing and eat the sandwiches she and her mom had brought from Sammy's Deli next door.

How she wished she could go back to those simpler days. Life had seemed so easy then. Her dad had seemed like a bonafide superhero. To Laurel, but also to the townspeople of Appleman's Gap. His great-grandfather had founded the town in 1876, back when America was celebrating being a country for just one century and wounds from the Civil War were all too fresh.

As the story goes, Chester Dane had moved west from the mountains along the Tennessee-North Carolina border in pursuit of Faye, the woman who would become his wife. They'd met when he'd made a delivery to her parents on their farm in Nashville. Wishing to be with Faye but also to carry on his own family's tradition of growing apples, Chester found a spot as close to Nashville as possible that was hilly enough and high enough elevation for the fruit to grow and mature. A tenacious man by nature, he brought seeds from home and got busy planting an orchard, his new bride looking on as her belly grew right along with the saplings. Soon, other settlers followed suit and the town was officially founded in 1883, named for the space near the Cumberland Plateau where orchards now thrive.

Old Chester was a legend around these parts. There was still an apple festival every fall in his honor.

The Danes that came after him enjoyed an elevated status as a result of his efforts. And no one made use of that status more than Cornelius Dane. When he'd run for town sheriff, he'd been a shoo-in, getting elected by a landslide. The entire town was still mourning his loss.

"Here you go," the young receptionist said, scurrying into the room and dropping acetaminophen and a bottle of water on the table in front of Laurel.

"Thank you," she said wearily. She tried to take the items

from his grip, but he fumbled them too fast. "I didn't get your name."

He shrank back, shoving a hand through his blonde hair and pausing just long enough to reply. "Wilson. I mean Matt. Matt Wilson."

"Nice to meet you, Matt Wilson," she said sincerely. "This will really hit the spot." Laurel didn't see many faces at the station she recognized anymore. She figured it was in her best interest to make friends.

"Good. I'm glad," he mumbled. "Sounds like you had a tough day."

"That's putting it mildly," she replied as she swallowed a couple of pills and washed them down with water. "But my day wasn't half as bad as that poor baby's. I'm sick about him being taken. I should have been able to keep him safe."

Matt softened, then sat down beside Laurel and took her hand in his. "Now, don't go beating yourself up over that," he implored. "My momma always says that we're only human, after all."

"Tell that to the baby's mother, who happens to be my closest friend," Laurel said, tears threatening to reveal themselves. She bit them back.

"It's true," he continued. "Hold your head high. From what I hear, you did an exemplary job noting your surroundings, which gave our officers enough information to find you."

Laurel smiled half heartedly. "But not enough information to find the baby."

"Not yet," Matt said. "The key word is *yet*. They'll find him. I know they will."

Laurel didn't believe his assurances. What did this kid

know, anyway? He was probably too wet behind the ears to actually understand the odds of finding a missing child as the hours ticked by. Sometimes, she wished she didn't know the odds, either. This was certainly one of those times.

Just then, an imposing figure appeared at the door.

Matt jumped, then dropped Laurel's hand and hurried out of the room. "Have faith," he mouthed on his way out.

If only it were that simple, she thought.

She nodded appreciatively, then appraised the man in the doorway. He was as big as a linebacker, and muscular like one, too. His well-defined physique was visible under his tailored dress shirt, neat belt, and pants that seemed to cling in all the right places. Laurel liked to think of herself as immune to the charms of such a man. At least, she didn't let herself succumb to any such charms when she was on duty. Especially not when there was important business at hand like informing Sarah about her son's disappearance and finding baby Jasper.

"Hello, Ms. Dane," the man said as he entered the room and sat down in a chair across from Laurel. A pair of male underlings followed closely behind—one older and gray haired, the other who looked like a smaller version of the big guy. They found seats as well, then proceeded to open note pads and ready their pens.

"It's Agent Dane, with the Bureau," she corrected. "And what? Don't you people have any women that work here?"

She asked to make a point, but she knew law enforcement was a male-dominated profession. She was used to being the only woman in the room. Although, if she did see another woman anytime soon, she wouldn't hesitate to ask to borrow a hair tie. Laurel's long, wavy hair was a pain to wrangle on a good day. Now, after being matted in the trunk, it felt like broom straw on her head.

The big man smiled politely, but didn't address her remark about demographics of the station's employees. "Right. Agent Dane. I have your file. I know who you are."

"Is that why we're here, instead of out looking for the baby? I'd like to get a move on, if it's all right with you."

He sighed, then leaned against the back of his chair. "More like that's why we're in this room instead of back in interrogation."

Laurel stiffened. "Am I a suspect?"

"Easy girl," he quipped. "Let's not get ahead of ourselves."

Laurel immediately disliked his tone. She was a full grown woman in her early thirties. Not to mention, she had most likely achieved more in her career with the Bureau than this clown had in small-town Tennessee. He was the epitome of a big fish in a little pond. She hated pompous men like that.

She held her tongue, though, realizing that sparring with this guy would only hamper her efforts to get things done.

"How would you like to proceed?" she asked calmly, measuring her words.

"Let's begin again. Seems we got off on the wrong foot. I'm Detective Josh Nolan. Appleman's Gap P.D. How are you feeling?"

At that, Laurel scoffed. His concern was fake. That much was obvious. He looked away briefly as he asked the question, a classic sign of insincerity.

"What?" Detective Nolan asked.

She collected herself, forcing the best acting job she could muster. "I'm sore, but okay. Thank you for asking. Officer

Wilson was kind enough to bring me some painkillers. They should be kicking in soon."

"Good man," Nolan said approvingly. One of his minions —the young one—nodded his agreement.

"Is Sarah on her way here? Or should we go to her home?" Laurel asked, cutting to the chase. "I'll just need a ride with one of your officers because my car is ... well, you know."

Detective Nolan pursed his lips. "Sarah is your friend?"

"Yes."

"The mother of the baby who was in the car with you?"

"Yes," Laurel replied, "But you already know that. I explained it all on the phone to Officer Martin. I assume you've read that transcript. Why ask again?"

"How about you let me do my job?" he asked.

She raised her brows, tempted to make an "easy girl" remark. Instead, she exercised restraint. "My apologies. Yes, Sarah is the mother of baby Jasper, who was kidnapped. We'd been at the holiday market when a man grabbed me and threw me into the trunk of my car. Baby Jasper was already buckled into his car seat in the back. Sarah had returned to the store to retrieve a forgotten scarf. Thankfully or not, depending on how you look at it, she was left there unharmed."

"And you're expecting to see her ... here?"

The minions scribbled furiously on their notepads as if Detective Nolan had said something profound.

"Well, yes," Laurel said. "I want to be the one to tell her what happened. It's the right thing to do. She'll take it better coming from me."

Detective Nolan scratched his chiseled jawline and

narrowed his eyes. "The thing is ... We don't know what your involvement is with the kidnapper. You're not even a local. We have to conduct a thorough investigation, and that means considering the possibility that you were working with this man."

So much for the royal treatment.

"You've got to be kidding," Laurel said. "I'm beaten up. You think I'd fake my injuries? Or worse ... that I'd allow myself to be harmed to make it look convincing? That's ridiculous. I'm an agent with the federal government, for God's sake. They don't let just anyone wear that badge. Do you have any idea what kind of vetting I've been through? What kind of training?"

She could hardly believe this. It made zero sense. Never in a million years would Laurel have expected to be questioned as a suspect at any police department, let alone her dad's. And now she was, apparently, going to be kept away from Sarah. Some idiot would probably break the news to her instead. Laurel was devastated.

"Am I under arrest?" she asked, beads of sweat beginning to form on her brow.

Three

BEFORE DETECTIVE NOLAN COULD ANSWER, another man burst through the door, making it bang against the wall behind him. This man was big and muscular, too, and the detective instantly recognized the newcomer as his superior. He stood quickly.

"Chief Tate, I wasn't expecting you." Detective Nolan said. He tried unsuccessfully to hide the nervousness in his voice, but mostly, he seemed surprised.

"Tate?" Laurel mumbled. Her eyes grew as wide as saucers when she realized that she knew the ... *chief.* She could hardly believe it.

"I'll take over here," Chief Brad Tate said. He had nothing but a smartphone in his hands, his short, black hair damp like he'd just stepped out of the shower. "That'll be all, Detective."

Laurel remained silent, working to process what was happening and wondering how any of this made sense. Brad Tate should be in D.C. where she left him, not Appleman's Gap.

Detective Nolan opened his mouth to protest, but thought better of it. With a dutiful nod, he tightened his jaw and motioned for his underlings to follow. "Looks like we're done, boys," he said. It was obvious that he was miffed, but no one cared.

Posturing and perceived slights were par for the course in a small-town police department. They were just as much a part of the culture as talking down to women and overblown male egos. Except that Brad Tate wasn't anything like that. At least, he wasn't before. Had he changed?

No, surely not.

When the door was closed again and Laurel and Brad were alone, she used every ounce of her willpower to keep herself from rushing into his arms. She loved this man, like no other. They'd been together for nearly six years. They'd only recently broken up after the death of Laurel's father because she'd wanted time to focus on herself. She hadn't shared her doubts with anyone besides Brad, but she'd been considering a career adjustment. That's why she'd taken an extended leave over the holidays. To think things through.

Brad pulled a chair around the table and sat next to Laurel. "I came as soon as I heard," he said. "I'm sorry it took me so long."

She was still shocked. It was hard to find words.

Suddenly self conscious about her bruises, Laurel tilted her head so that her hair covered one bloody cheek. She didn't want Brad to see her weak like this. At the same time, though, he was the one person—other than her late father—whom she felt safe enough with to actually lean on.

"What are you doing here?" she asked.

"I heard your name come across the radio and got here right away."

"I mean, what are you doing *here* ... in Appleman's Gap? You're the new chief?" she asked.

Brad had been to Tennessee with Laurel many times over the years to visit, and he'd been by her side at her dad's memorial service just months ago. He'd held her hand as the family had scattered the man's ashes. Sure, Brad had often talked about how he'd love to leave the rat race that was Washington D.C. and move somewhere with a slower pace. Laurel never thought he'd actually do it. Especially not in her hometown of Appleman's Gap.

He smiled broadly. "That I am. You think your dad would approve? I hope so. I work every day to make him proud and honor his memory. He was one of the best men I've ever known."

"He'd like to hear you say that," she replied.

Brad smiled again in that easy way of his. "I dig it here. I'm making friends. Even got a dog."

"You did?" Laurel asked, her eyes lighting up.

They'd discussed adopting a dog, but their crazy work schedules in D.C. barely allowed time for them to see each other, let alone take proper care of a pet.

"I did," he beamed. "A spotted girl with ruffly fur and big eyes who is black, white, and brown. She's a beauty. She's only two years-old. She belonged to an old woman who passed away last summer. Relatives couldn't keep her for long, so I stepped in. I think she misses a female presence though. The poor pup seems to be grieving."

"Aww, sweet girl," Laurel said, aware that she had completely dropped the Agent Dane persona and was being her personal, genuine self with the man she loved. "What's her name?"

"Lilly."

Brad searched for a picture of the pooch on his phone. When he found one, he showed Laurel proudly.

"I'm so happy for you," she said softly. "You're living your dream, I suppose. Good for you for making it happen. You'd better believe I want to hear all of the details, just as soon as I get myself out of this current predicament."

His expression became more serious, and he took off his leather bomber jacket and slung it over the back of his chair. He was dressed in civilian clothes. He must not have had time to put on his uniform. "About that, don't worry. I'm going to take your statement, then I'm taking you home to Maureen's house. I already called her and let her know that we'd be along soon."

"You called my mom?" Laurel was surprised, but not unhappy. "Wait, did she know you're the new chief? She must have. That stinker. She didn't breathe a word to me."

"She promised not to tell."

Laurel smiled, making a mental note to find out more about this chain of events later, too. She had so many questions.

"You might want to check with your detective before you go any further. He made it sound like I'm a suspect," she explained.

"Oh, yeah?"

"It was a short conversation, but yeah," she replied. "He said they can't be sure that I wasn't connected to the kidnapper. I wanted to break the news to Sarah and to help with the investigation. He made it sound like I wouldn't be able to do either. Can you get me access?"

Brad hesitated. "I don't know. I can get you home tonight, but I'm not certain what tomorrow will bring."

"That sounds vague and well, disturbing, if I'm being honest," she replied. "Doesn't my background speak for itself? I'm not a criminal."

"I know that. You know that. But it's complicated."

Laurel shook her head. "It's actually not complicated at all, Brad. What aren't you telling me?"

The room suddenly felt too small. Too quiet. Brad wasn't jumping in to reassure Laurel, and she didn't like it. "Look" he said, "I'll take you home to your mom's house, and then I'll inform Sarah myself. Okay?"

"We're not exactly interchangeable," Laurel said. "Sarah knows all about our breakup. She knows we haven't spoken recently. And besides, I'm the one who should have kept her baby safe. It was on my watch. It's my fault."

Hearing Laurel blame herself visibly pained Brad. He reached out to put an arm around her, but she shrugged him off.

"By that standard, I'm the police chief in this town, so it's ultimately my responsibility. I should have done something to prevent the carjacking from happening in the first place. My officers should have gotten there sooner," he said.

"Nonsense, and you know it."

Laurel's head began to pound. Those painkillers weren't up to the challenge. This was all too much. She could only imagine what her mom would have to say about this mess. Her rowdy and opinionated siblings would, no doubt, chime in, too.

Brad put a firm hand on Laurel's forearm. This, she allowed. "I need you to trust me, okay? Right now, it's that simple. Let's get you home. Then I'll inform Sarah, and I swear to everything that's holy I'll pull out all the stops to find that baby. My team and I won't rest until he's home safe."

"And tomorrow? What about me?" she asked. "It's a holiday weekend. I'd like my name cleared as soon as possible so that I can assist with the investigation."

"I'll come by before lunch and give you an update. I promise."

Laurel didn't like this. She wished she had done any of a thousand things differently so Baby Jasper would be safe at home with his mother, not in the car with a dangerous madman. She hoped the child was warm.

That reminded her of Bear, Sarah's dog, and she thought maybe she could help track him down and get him to safety.

"Actually," she said, "can I borrow your car?"

Brad looked confused. "I mean it, Laurel, you have to leave this investigation alone. At least, for now."

"No. I know," she said. "But Sarah's dog was in the back-seat. He took off when the kidnapper opened the door. If I can't help in any other way, maybe I can find him. He must be terrified out there. And cold. He'll be hungry soon, if he isn't already. He doesn't strike me as a dog who would last long on the streets."

Brad didn't see the harm in letting Laurel poke around for the dog. "Fine," he said. "But do not disturb the crime scene. Got it? My deputies are still processing it."

Laurel grinned, relieved that she could do something. The last thing she wanted was to sit uselessly on her hands.

This plan had the added benefit of allowing her to avoid

her family for a while longer. She wasn't ready for that drama just yet. They were probably all riled up, gathered at their mom's house to fret over the events of the evening. They didn't seem to understand Laurel's need to serve and protect. They chalked it up to a need to be like their dad and get his approval. None of them realized it was so much more complex than that.

Brad stood. "Come on, then. We need to swing by my place so I can get my cruiser."

Laurel followed him, resigned to the concession that would allow her to help out in a small way. She'd take it one step at a time from there. She waved goodbye to Matt Wilson as she walked through the familiar front door and into the cold night air.

Four

"YOU BOUGHT A TRUCK?" Laurel asked as Brad unlocked the shiny new vehicle with a beep and opened the passenger door for her.

The truck was American made in a deep, metallic blue. Fitting for a police officer.

Laurel wouldn't normally allow a colleague to open her car door, but with Brad, it was a habit. When they'd dated, she had worked for the F.B.I and he had been a detective with the Metropolitan Police Department. The city was big enough that their paths didn't cross professionally, so they were free to act like any other couple while off duty.

Old habits were hard to break.

"Sure did. It was my first big purchase when I moved. You like her?" Brad asked.

"Now you're referring to your automobile as her?" Laurel asked as she climbed in and buckled her seatbelt. "Gag me."

He chuckled. "Maybe I'm trying to fit in with my new community. How am I doing so far?"

She raised her brows. "Not too bad."

She hated to admit it, but the truck and Brad's easy-going charm would serve him well in Appleman's Gap. Her dad had thrived, thanks to much the same.

They chatted like old friends during the short ride down the main drag in town, both happy to be in each other's company again. It was a relief for Laurel. A stark contrast to the way she'd spent the earlier part of the evening.

"Hey, are you hungry?" he asked as they approached the local diner.

She was starving, but she hated to eat when Baby Jasper was missing. Brad could tell what she was thinking, so he put a hand on her forearm again while turning into the parking lot. Once more, Laurel allowed this friendly touch.

She wanted to be strong and tough, like an F.B.I. agent should, but she was also tired and traumatized. She needed comfort and companionship, like any other person would. Especially given the memories the carjacking had stirred up.

"My deputies are on it," Brad said. "You have to eat. If you don't take care of yourself, you won't be able to take care of anyone else."

She nodded reluctantly. "You're right."

He parked the truck, then winked and patted her arm. "Stay here. I'll grab us something to go and we can eat at my place. You can meet Lilly, before you head out to look for Bear."

Laurel nodded. "Okay, if you'll do me a favor first."

Brad twisted toward her in his seat and leaned against the headrest. The pose was a sweet one. It reminded Laurel of seeing him in bed, looking over at her from his pillow.

"For you? Anything," he said.

"Get someone to update Sarah. She shouldn't have to wait."

"I completely agree," he said. "She knows about the carjacking, of course. She came out of the holiday market to find that your car had disappeared, but she hasn't been updated on your safe return …"

"And her baby's further disappearance," Laurel said, finishing his sentence.

"Right."

Laurel thought about asking if she could call Sarah, using Brad's phone, but she decided against it because someone should really deliver this news in person. The phone she had gotten for her mom that she used to place the 9-1-1 call had been admitted as evidence.

"I'll send a couple of my best guys out to talk to her, and I'll follow up later. Okay? Then you can eat with a clear conscience."

"Oh, I'm far from having a clear conscience," she replied. "I know what you mean, though. It's a start."

Brad nodded, then got out of the truck and placed the call as he walked into the diner. Laurel watched him through the side mirror out her window. He hadn't asked what she wanted to eat, because he already knew what she liked. The relationship between them had always been effortless. It made her wonder now why she'd ever broken up with him. Perhaps doing so had been a big mistake.

That's what happens when you're grieving, she supposed. She'd been told not to make any major life decisions for a full year after the loss of her dad. It hadn't even been half of that yet and she'd broken up with a man she truly loved and was thinking about leaving her job at the Bureau. For what, she wasn't sure. Maybe she'd become a private investigator. She had a certain set of skills that might as well be put to use, but she was growing weary of the politics and red tape inherent in the field.

Not so long ago, Laurel had been on an entirely different career path, anyway. In college, she had been a music performance major who played orchestral French horn. She had unmistakable talent, proven by the number of full scholarship offers she'd received out of high school. She chose to attend the University of Maryland, College Park, where she thoroughly enjoyed her time practicing, studying, and performing on stage in various ensembles. Something else had nagged at her, though, and in her junior year, she decided to add a double major in criminal justice.

Maybe she truly had wanted to be like her dad. Or maybe she had felt guilty possessing such an obvious talent when her younger siblings were struggling. Whatever the case, at that critical juncture, she diversified her training and had begun to consider a career in law enforcement.

"So much for that decision," Laurel mumbled to herself as she thought about it. "Maybe I should have stuck with the horn. And Brad Tate."

Lately, she'd been wondering if she had steered her life in the wrong direction.

After college, she didn't think she was ready for graduate school and she didn't want to teach music to kids, either, so she auditioned for and joined the United States Air Force Band. The four years she spent as an active duty musician were some of the best she'd ever experienced. Being part of the premiere band allowed her to travel all over the world, as well as to perform locally in the Washington, D.C. metro area. It was a dream, really. Nothing compared to the pride Laurel had felt wearing her Air Force uniform and using her talent to entertain. She could hardly get through a performance of "America the Beautiful" without breaking into full-body goose bumps.

She was still deep in thought when Brad returned with a big to-go bag and a couple of paper cups.

"Did I ever tell you the story of how I was recruited to the Bureau?" she asked as she took the drinks from him and secured them in the center console.

Brad's door dinged to be closed as he took straws and napkins out of his jacket pocket and stuffed them into an open spot on the console. "You mean the one where they needed you to spy on a foreign diplomat while posing as an innocent horn player?" he asked.

"Yeah," she replied, "but did I tell you the details?"

He closed the door, then looked into Laurel's eyes. "Tell me again."

She smiled as Brad started up the ignition and pulled back onto the two-lane road. "They approached me after a concert we'd just performed on the National Mall one summer evening. Two guys in suits and sunglasses took me by the arms and asked if we could have a private conversation. I thought I was about to get mugged, until the conductor gave me a nod to let me know he was in on it."

"That must have been unnerving."

"It sure was. The agents had already cleared their plan with my superiors. All they needed was my cooperation and they'd have the perfect espionage agent who would blend in seamlessly," she explained. "Can you imagine? It felt like a scene out of a movie. I half expected someone to jump out from behind a column and tell me that it was some sort of prank."

"No such luck, huh?" Brad asked.

"Nope," she continued. "It ended up so much more fun. Dangerous, but fun. I miss that spark. That feeling of being needed."

Brad pursed his lips. It seemed like he had plenty to say, but didn't want to open old wounds. There was much to focus on in the present moment. His place wasn't far, so he chose to focus on that. He knew he could distract Laurel with Lilly. His ex-girlfriend was a sucker for cute dogs.

"My humble abode is right up here," he said as he pointed to a bungalow nestled into the hillside.

It was hard to make out details in the dark, but Brad's two-story house featured siding stained a warm brown with a craftsman front door and a big, airy front porch. Warm light glowed from lamps inside.

"My God," Laurel said, "it's gorgeous. Are you renting?"

He shook his head proudly. "No, I own it. You told me to go and live my life. To find what would make me feel settled and accomplished. Here I am."

"Wow," she said simply.

This was a lot for Laurel to take in. She had sort of hoped that Brad would be there waiting when she had healed and was ready to resume their relationship. She hadn't expected him to make such big moves for himself. She couldn't blame him, though. He had asked her to marry him. Not only had she turned his proposal down, she had broken up with him and told him to go out and find his own happiness. He had done that, and then some.

Brad parked the truck in the driveway on the side of the

house, then grabbed the bag of food and climbed out. "Come on," he said. "Lilly will be glad to meet you."

Laurel carried the cups, straws and napkins, then followed along. It felt strange not to have a handbag. That was still in her car. She walked carefully on decking under string lights to enter the house from the back, which by the way, was just as charming as curb appeal from the front.

It was all enchanting, until a noise startled her. She jumped, her nerves raw after the events of the evening. The sound was a door opening, that much was certain. Laurel looked to Brad for his reaction. Surprisingly, he wasn't alarmed.

"Hey there, Jamie," he said casually as he waved to a beautiful blonde woman who had just emerged from the building on the back of his property.

"Hey you," she replied with a mischievous smile. "Who's your guest?"

Laurel's jaw dropped. Immediately, she could tell that Jamie must be staying there, and that she and Brad were more than friends.

Five

"I CAN'T DEAL with this right now," Laurel said as she entered Brad's house and closed the door hard behind her. "I should go."

Before Laurel could make good on that, Lilly bounded out of a bedroom and greeted her with insistent yet polite requests to be petted.

"Meet my baby girl," Brad said.

Under these circumstances, the phrase stung. Laurel didn't like the thought of Brad having any other "girl" than her. It was unreasonable. She knew that. She'd been the one to break up with him and push him away. She didn't have any idea that she'd be pushing him into the arms of someone else. A blonde, beautiful someone else.

Laurel mentally kicked herself so that she could focus on the dog in front of her. She stooped down to Lilly's level and stroked the pup's silky little head.

"Hello, Lilly," she managed. "You're a pretty girl, aren't you? I hear you like women."

That reminder also stung. Brad must have discovered that

the dog prefers women by way of seeing her reaction to Jamie. Meaning Jamie has been in his house. Probably in his bed.

Damn him.

Laurel closed her eyes and shook her head, then stood as soon as she'd collected herself. "Lilly is great," she said, "but I need to go. Will you call my mom and ask her to pick me up at the grocery around the corner?"

"I thought we were having dinner, and I thought you were borrowing my truck to look for Bear. What's happening?"

"Things have changed," Laurel replied. "Send someone else to look for Bear. Maybe Jamie will eat my dinner. Thanks anyway."

With that, she turned around and left the house, taking quick steps toward the road out front. Brad opened the door to call her back, but she didn't respond. She was overwhelmed with too many emotions at once. She had never imagined that *her* Brad would move on with someone else. Certainly not so quickly. And in her hometown, no less. It was a cruel twist of fate. So, instead of facing the situation head on like a mature adult, Laurel put one foot in front of the other and walked the half mile or so to the grocery store.

She only had to wait about ten minutes until her mom, Maureen Dane, pulled up in her trademark gold Buick.

"Well, don't you look fit to be tied," Maureen said as Laurel climbed into the passenger seat.

The woman was known for her plethora of Southern sayings that kept everyone around her entertained. Her hair was already in curlers for the night and she wore a plush pink robe over her nightgown. She'd been sad since Cornelius died, but she hadn't let it change her character.

"You could say that," Laurel replied.

"What in the world happened?"

"Brad didn't tell you?" she asked.

Maureen shook her head.

"Just drive, then," Laurel said. "I've had *the* worst day. I want to get home and go to bed. I'll tell you all about it tomorrow."

The next morning, sun shone low through the edges of the drawn curtain as a new day made its appearance. It took Laurel a few minutes to orient herself and remember what had happened. She'd been so tired the night before that she'd climbed into bed at her mom's house and fallen asleep without so much as changing her clothes. There was still blood on her cotton shirt, alongside dirt and grime from the trunk.

"Ugh," she mumbled as she stretched and rolled onto her back.

"That bad?" a voice asked from the other side of the room.

Laurel startled, leaping out of bed and mentally searching for a weapon. Soon enough, her brain caught up and she realized there wasn't a threat. It was only her younger sister, Maggie, who was camped out on a recliner with a laptop and a bottle of green juice.

Magnolia Dane—Maggie, for short—was an internet entrepreneur who could work from anywhere. Although, granted, Laurel wasn't completely sure what kind of work she actually did. Maggie was still unattached as far as a significant other went, so she could show up for duties like watching her big sister sleep. Maureen must have told her that Laurel'd had a rough time.

That's the kind of thing that happens in a big family and a small town. Everyone knows your business.

"Maggie? What are you doing here?"

Maggie chucked, her strawberry blonde hair and freckles glistening in the morning light. It reminded Laurel of when her sister was a kid. She'd always had a child-like innocence about her. "Are you creeped out right now?"

"Kind of," Laurel confirmed. "Let me guess. Mom put you up to this."

"Right-o, big sister," Maggie said. "She didn't want the golden child to become too sad or traumatized."

"Stop it," Laurel said, bristling at the label. "I'm no such thing."

"Okay, keep telling yourself that."

It wasn't a new sentiment among Laurel's siblings. She had been the only one to move away from Tennessee, and her parents had always made a big production when she returned home to visit. One of their brothers, Mikey, lived in Knoxville, but that was just a couple of hours away. He made it home to visit regularly. Maggie, their youngest sister, Hazel, and their brother, Ryan, had all stayed put in Appleman's Gap. Laurel had often thought they'd do better to move away and spread their wings, but she had tried to understand the appeal of living near family. There were advantages.

"So, what's on the agenda today, boss?" Maggie asked.

Laurel wished her sister wouldn't treat her like that. The passive aggressive digs to indicate that Laurel was better than the others actually hurt.

"Can we drop this routine?" Laurel asked. "You have no idea what I went through yesterday. Seriously, Sis. Please."

Maggie raised her hands in the air, her short nails looking

clean and natural. "Okay, okay. What are you doing on this Saturday? Need a ride?"

Laurel smiled her thanks. "My car was taken, so yeah, a ride—or two, or three—would be great. At least until I can get a rental. Does your schedule permit?"

Maggie shrugged. "Sure. I have to pick up a piece of furniture out in Carthage this afternoon, but otherwise, I'm free."

"Oh, for your condo, or ...?"

"To sell," Maggie replied. "My condo is already full to the brim."

Laurel was happy for a chance to learn a little more about her sister's life. It had been one of the items on her mental to-do list when she'd decided to take an extended leave over the holidays. She wanted to know all of her siblings better.

"You sell online?" Laurel asked.

"That's right. I sell all kinds of things—furniture, clothing, jewelry. I buy it cheap when I find a deal, then I fix it up if needed, package it up all pretty, sell, and deliver or ship to the buyer. You might be surprised. It's a lucrative business, as long as I don't take my foot off the gas for too long."

Maggie was a free-spirited type. Almost a hippie, really. She might have fit in better in East Nashville, or even in Asheville, North Carolina. But she liked Appleman's Gap, and she stuck around. Laurel admired her for piecing together a business that worked. The flexible schedule must be nice.

"Makes sense," Laurel replied. "I wondered exactly what you did on the internet all the time. I'm happy to learn the details."

Maggie nodded. Laurel couldn't tell for certain how comfortable her sister was in sharing, but she considered their conversation a good start.

Laurel opened the curtains on the four small windows in the bedroom, letting the light in. It was a bright day for November, which she appreciated. She hoped it was a good sign that they'd make progress in baby Jasper's case. Of course, it was Laurel's case, too. She was a victim. She wanted the guy caught, all right, but she only considered herself as an afterthought. It was the baby who was on her mind.

With the curtains open, the sisters had an unobstructed view of the rolling hills and apple orchard that had made a name for their family in Appleman's Gap. It was beautiful, if Laurel did say so herself. Even though she'd grown up here and had seen this view a million times, it never got old.

Maureen still oversaw the business, and Hazel tended the orchard gift shop and coordinated the vacation rental cabins on the property. Otherwise, though, the Dane family was hands off when it came to the workings of the orchard. Long ago, they had hired reliable people to take those duties off their hands. It was a good thing, because it was more work than even the large Dane family could handle on their own. Most visitors to the orchard had no clue the amount of man hours that went into keeping the business running.

"Sure is pretty, isn't it?" Maggie asked.

Laurel paused, realizing she was deep in thought. The scenic views had stolen her attention. "Beautiful. We're lucky to call this place home."

Maggie nodded. She looked like she wanted to say a long piece, but she kept it simple. "Sure are."

Taking a breath, Laurel began to think about the day ahead of her. She wanted to get involved in the investigation, but wasn't sure how to manage that when the local police were acting guarded. She needed to call her Special Agent in Charge, Jimmy Paulson, to check in. That much was certain.

"Okay, I'm going to get cleaned up. Then I need to call my boss to check in. How about we go from there when I hear what he has to say?"

"No problemo," Maggie replied. "I'll get out of your hair while you shower."

Laurel smiled her thanks as she began to pull clean clothes out of the closet. She had unpacked her suitcase the week before, knowing she'd be staying a while.

"Hey, Maggie," Laurel said as her sister was heading out the door.

"Yeah?"

"Thank you."

"You're welcome," Maggie said. "Keep talking nice to me and I might even make you a turkey sandwich from the Thanksgiving leftovers."

She winked, then closed the door, leaving Laurel alone.

LAUREL WAS at her mom's big kitchen table, showered, dressed, and eating leftovers, when the text from Brad came through on her mom's phone. Laurel spotted the message before Maureen had a chance.

> Tell Laurel, please … a new development needs my attention. Will catch up with her later.

"Of course," Laurel mumbled. "Figures."

"Is that from Brad?" Maureen asked.

Maureen was semi-retired and didn't typically work on weekends. That meant she had plenty of time to hover over Laurel.

"Yeah, he was supposed to come by today to talk to me about the kidnapping case," Laurel explained. "I'm afraid Brad's the only real friend I have on the local force, except for a chatty desk guy who probably doesn't possess the power to do much on his own."

"Does something have Brad's knickers in a knot?"

Maureen asked between bites. "Both of you were acting strange last night."

As promised, Maggie had made them all turkey sandwiches from the ample Thanksgiving leftovers. She had piled mashed potatoes, stuffing, gravy, cranberry sauce, spinach, mayonnaise, and Dijon mustard along with the warmed turkey on sourdough bread. It tasted delicious, hitting the spot for Laurel who was starving after having skipped dinner the evening before.

"I don't know about that, but he says he'll catch up to me later. Something must have happened," Laurel said. "A new development."

Laurel didn't want to get into her mixed emotions about seeing Brad for the first time since the breakup. She also didn't care to talk about Jamie. Maureen and Maggie probably knew things as a result of living in this small town where Brad was the new chief. Laurel wasn't sure her heart could take any more surprises. Not yet, anyway.

"If your dad were here ..." Maureen began, a wistful look in her eyes.

Maggie piped up, interrupting their mom. "Hey, want me to look up a police scanner and see what I can find out?"

"You can do that?" Laurel asked.

They were both keen to leave talk of their dad alone. They were all still torn up about his death, but their mom was the one who had a tendency to dwell on the subject. Not that anyone blamed her. Maureen and Cornelius had been married for nearly forty years. That's a long time to get used to someone being around, day in and day out. Maureen was, understandably, struggling with her life partner's absence. But her kids thought it best to keep her focused on the here and now. That and the future. They didn't want her to turn out like those sad saps who give up on a life of their own once their spouses die. Maureen had plenty of life left in her. She was too spunky a personality for them to think otherwise.

"With a few clicks, yep, I can," Maggie replied.

Laurel raised her brows. Listening to a police scanner wasn't a bad idea. Maybe someone would be talking about whatever this new development was. Maybe it could give her a lead to go on. She was desperate to do something to help, especially because the missing baby belonged to her best friend, Sarah.

"Do it," Laurel said, pushing her long hair behind one ear, a sign that she was ready to get down to business.

Shrugging as if to say "no sweat," Maggie opened her laptop and started clicking. In less than a minute, the local public safety radio transmission was playing through her speaker. It was muffled at first, but soon a male deputy's voice sounded clear. Maggie leaned back in her chair, satisfied with her own resourcefulness.

"Who's your favorite sibling?" Maggie asked.

"You, of course," Maureen answered on Laurel's behalf. "Bless your heart."

She smiled at her daughters as she used a pretty cloth napkin to wipe mayonnaise from the corners of her mouth. Maureen had always loved seasonal decor, and the brilliant autumn colors on the cloth napkins suited her style perfectly.

"Okay, okay," Laurel said, leaning closer to hear the garbled sound. "Now hush, you two."

They all looked hopeful as they listened. It took a few minutes for anything of substance to be heard, but when it happened, it was cause for immediate action.

A male voice announced himself as an Appleman's Gap police department deputy and asked for backup at a waterfront restaurant near Hillside Marina. He was on the scene where an employee had found an abandoned infant car seat in the men's bathroom. Based on the description provided, Laurel suspected the seat was baby Jasper's.

She wondered if this was the development Brad had been referring to. Although, based on the timing, perhaps there was something else. That only made her more eager to get involved, somehow.

"I've got to go," Laurel said, standing and grabbing her sister's keys from a silver bowl on the entryway table. The metal clanked pleasantly. "Can you drive me, Maggie? Or can I take your SUV?"

Maggie didn't hesitate. "Go on. Get. I'll be here with Mom today. If I need to go anywhere, I'm sure she'll let me drive ol' Goldie."

Maureen nodded her agreement. "Be safe, dear."

Laurel blew an air kiss to her mom and little sister as she picked up her handbag, coat, and scarf from a hook near the front door. "Thank you, Maggie. I'll be sure to have it back before you need to get the furniture from Carthage. What time is that?"

Maggie waved a hand in the air. "Get out of here. Goldie can get that job done. It's just an end table that I have to fetch. I don't reckon there would be any trouble fitting it into the back seat of Mom's Buick."

"You're the best," Laurel cooed. "Thanks again."

Once outside, Laurel made a beeline down the brick stairs and along the winding walkway to where her sister's Toyota 4Runner was parked in the driveway. The air was cold and there was still snow on the ground, but the sun was doing its best to shine over the rolling hills. A bright red winter bird sat perched on the fence line over toward the orchard. Laurel had to admit, the whole scene was picturesque. She had a mission to focus on, though. As she unlocked the vehicle and climbed in, she began reviewing a mental checklist of what to expect at the scene.

Being an F.B.I. agent, she wasn't familiar with all of the procedures that a small-town police force would follow in a situation like this. By the time the Bureau got involved and took over a scene, the basics had already been done. It occurred to her that she should probably learn, if she wanted to become a private investigator.

Too bad Laurel couldn't call Brad and ask him. He'd be happy to share details about crime scene process and procedure. The two of them had always shared things like that with each other. Technically, she could call him—if she had a phone—but she was still mad. Or confused. Or something. She wasn't sure how to describe her feelings. All she knew was that seeing him had stirred something deep within her. It had awakened sentiments that she'd buried due to her grief. Being blindsided by Jamie had been an unpleasant turn of events.

Laurel had always believed she could trust Brad. Now, she wasn't so sure. What secrets was he hiding?

Detective Nolan sure seemed to have it out for her. If it were up to him, Laurel would probably be arrested. For what, she wasn't entirely sure.

That reminded her, she hadn't had a chance to call Agent Paulson in D.C. yet. Protocol stated that she needed to inform her superior if she were involved in any legal or police incident. She needed to place that call soon, before someone like

Detective Nolan beat her to it. She'd be forced out of the Bureau, if she weren't careful, and she wasn't ready to make a decision about leaving yet. She wanted to keep her options open while she sorted things out.

Laurel decided that her first order of business needed to be getting a new smartphone. Too many people were expecting to hear from her. She wanted to hurry to the scene where the baby seat had been found, but she knew she would be at a big disadvantage without a way to communicate. So, she stopped by the phone company store in town. Luckily, she didn't have to wait long. Within an hour, she exited the store with a shiny new phone for herself and another one for her mom to replace the gift that had been admitted into evidence. Laurel took a few idle minutes to power her new device up and send a text to key people letting them know about her new number. When she was finished, she put the 4Runner in gear and moved on with her day.

As she wound around the scenic two-lane road between the mountain and the river, approaching the spot where it opened to the lake and marina, Laurel wondered if she'd see Sarah today. She wanted desperately to see her friend, but the more time that passed without contact, the more apprehensive Laurel was about how to navigate the situation.

Sarah Peterson was the daughter of a single mother, and she didn't have siblings. Linda Peterson had done a fine job of raising Sarah and being a support to her, but Laurel couldn't help but feel bad for her friend now that she needed people to rally around her more than ever. Linda was the only relative Sarah had. Jasper's dad was in the picture, but Sarah and Owen Hobbs weren't serious. They'd never married or even committed to each other, instead settling into a sort of co-parent with benefits relationship. Laurel hoped Owen would step up and be there for Sarah during this ordeal. Someone must.

Surely, Sarah would blame Laurel for Baby Jasper's disappearance. She ought to. Laurel believed it was clearly her fault. It happened on her watch. Not to mention, she'd gotten away during the stop while the baby was taken again. As a law enforcement agent, Laurel had been taught to handle situations like the one she'd found herself in. She should have figured out a way to get the baby to safety.

Would Sarah ever forgive her? If the worst happened, probably not. That would be Laurel's cross to bear, but acceptance of that fact didn't make it any easier to swallow. It hurt, deep down in Laurel's chest, like a poisonous seed taking root. If it happened that way, it would haunt Laurel for the rest of her life.

As Hillside Marina came into view, Laurel immediately noticed the police presence in front of Jack and Jill's, cleverly named for the nursery rhyme where the siblings tumbled down a hill. Four squad cars and what looked like an unmarked cruiser sat perpendicular to the parking lines out front. The bathrooms were located on the back side of the building and had their own entrances that weren't accessible from inside the restaurant. Yellow police tape stretched around that entire end of the structure.

"Seems overkill for an abandoned baby seat, but okay," Laurel mused to herself.

Then she got out of the SUV, tucked her new phone into her back pocket, and made her move.

Seven

IT WAS LUNCHTIME, and the restaurant was busy. Laurel slid into a chair at an empty table where she had a good view of the comings and goings. Even though it was cold outside, the patio was comfortably warm, thanks to some surprisingly powerful heaters lining the edges of the space.

Jack and Jill's was one of the most popular restaurants in town, and they stayed open year-round. The scenic view of the lake against the hills was a draw for locals and tourists alike. Gazing at the water as it lapped gently against the rocks along the shore made Laurel relax. This place provided nature's therapy, and it was just one of many such locales in the area.

The crowd was buzzing with energy. Laurel got the sense that people were hanging around to catch a glimpse of what was happening out back. They were eating slowly, big eyed and curious. She didn't blame them. It wasn't often that Appleman's Gap saw this much action. Word had probably gotten out about the kidnapping. People were, understandably, afraid. Several parents sat huddled next to their kids as if they intended to keep them within arm's length. Laurel imagined that many more were huddled at home, watching news and social media for updates but too scared to leave the house.

She would have appreciated an update herself. To get one, she would need to be sneaky. But first, she wanted to reach out to her Special Agent in Charge at the Bureau, Jimmy Paulson. She might as well send him a text while she scoped out this scene and plotted her next move.

> Heads up: Was involved in an incident in my hometown of Appleman's Gap, TN last night. Will file a full report shortly. Hoping to assist with the local investigation.

She paused, then hit send without overthinking it. Jimmy would call to ask for details, no doubt. Laurel could ignore those calls, for a while anyway, but at least she had made contact.

A perky young woman with long braids approached her table. For a split second, Laurel wasn't sure if she was wait staff or not because she looked like she was freezing. Quickly, though, her Jack and Jill's name tag and pocketed apron gave her role away.

"Hi, there, I'm Kanesha," the woman said. "Can I get you something to drink?"

"Sure. Just water, please. Do you have bottles?"

Kanesha nodded, practically shivering, then darted back to the warmth of the kitchen. When she returned, Laurel couldn't resist asking a few questions.

"You look so cold," Laurel began, "I feel like I should give you my coat."

"Oh, I'm fine," the young woman said with a laugh as she set a bottle of water and a few napkins in front of Laurel. "I guess my roots are showing."

"What roots would those be?" Laurel asked.

Kanesha leaned down, like she was about to share a secret. "I'm from Florida. The always-warm part of Florida, down south. I moved here a few weeks ago and, I swear, the cold has already seeped deep into my bones."

Laurel smiled. "Ah, I get it. I'm sort of the opposite. I'm from here, but have been living in Washington, D.C. for years now. I think I've gotten used to the cold. I barely feel it anymore."

"I hope I'll get used to it," Kanesha said with a shiver. "And fast. Whew!" Moving on, she asked if Laurel had gotten a chance to look over the menu.

Laurel wasn't very hungry after the turkey sandwich, but she knew she needed to order something.

She decided that this young woman could be a good one to have as a friend. Kanesha was probably privy to the employee finding the infant seat, and she hadn't lived here long enough to have formed alliances with local police. In exchange, maybe Laurel could help her out by showing her around town, or something. She looked to be about Laurel's age.

"I'm not very hungry," Laurel explained. "My little sister made me a huge turkey sandwich with Thanksgiving leftovers. What do you have that's light?"

Kanesha looked at the menu over Laurel's shoulder and tapped a pen against her bottom lip as she thought. "You could do the Fisherman's Stew. I can bring you a cup, if you don't want a whole bowl. Or the Wedge Salad. They can even char the romaine for you, if you feel like being fancy."

"Wow," Laurel said. "Appleman's Gap has become so hip."

At that, they both laughed. The town was plenty of things—charming, quaint, cozy—but hip wasn't one of them. Not yet, anyway. Having spent time in more worldly places like South Florida and our nation's capital, both ladies knew it, too.

"They like to think they're hip," Kanesha replied with a chuckle. "I'm not so sure they are. I hear you have to drive to Nashville, if you want hip. Although, granted, with all the new people moving in around here, it might happen, in time."

Laurel nodded. Kanesha was right. New construction was at an all time high. The entire Nashville metro area was seeing record growth. Even in Appleman's Gap, located an hour or so from Nashville proper, new restaurants, stores, and apartment complexes were cropping up everywhere. Those from "old Appleman's Gap" were beginning to get frustrated about the traffic. They could be heard around town hemming and hawing about how long it now took to get anywhere, even though nothing took nearly as long as it did in big cities.

All the activity was a good thing for the Dane family's apple orchard, and Laurel intended to discuss it with her mom and siblings sometime soon. As far as she could tell, they were approaching a tipping point where they would either need to expand operations and get more involved in the day-to-day business, or cut ties and sell to someone willing to do the hard work they weren't. There was too much opportunity to ignore. Their orchard's prime location along the hillside, visible from the main drag through town, made them a prominent fixture, whether they liked it or not.

"Go ahead and get me both," Laurel said. "I'll have a cup of Fisherman's Stew and a Charred Romaine Wedge. I might as well walk on the wild side. I'll take the leftovers home to my mom, who probably hasn't eaten a charred wedge of lettuce before."

"Dressing?"

"You have ranch?"

Laurel closed the menu and handed it back to Kanesha.

"Sure do. Coming right up," the waitress said. "Can I get you anything else while you wait?"

Laurel decided it was time to ask a few pointed questions. Kanesha seemed friendly, and Laurel needed information. "Actually, yes," she said. "What can you tell me about all those police officers back there? What happened?"

Kanesha didn't hesitate. "One of the bus boys found a baby seat in the men's bathroom this morning. He thought it seemed odd, what with the missing baby and all. He told the manager, who called the police. And here they are." She made a sweeping gesture.

"I wonder what made him think the seat belonged to the missing baby," Laurel mused, fishing for details.

She hoped her face didn't reveal how much it pained her to remember her own involvement in the incident. She was still sore from being thrown in a trunk and beaten up last night.

"I don't know. Better to be safe, I guess?" Kanesha replied. "I mean, in Miami, it might not be that big of a deal. We have crime all the time. Lots of people coming and going.

Around here, though, I can see how it might give them a fright. I'm guessing babies don't get kidnapped every day."

"Definitely not every day," Laurel said.

Not wanting to push her luck, she thanked Kanesha and let the woman go to ring her order in. She'd ask more questions later.

As if on cue when Kanesha was gone, Laurel's phone rang. It was Jimmy Paulson, and even the ring sounded angry. She let it go to voicemail. The insistent ringing didn't stop, though, as Jimmy called right back—three times. When people at neighboring tables began to take notice, Laurel decided to bite the bullet and answer the man.

"Jimmy?" she asked, placing the phone to one ear and putting a finger in the other. They had known each other for a long time and were on a first-name basis.

Usually.

"Agent Dane!" he barked. If he'd been feeling happy, he would have called her Laurel. "Do you know what day it is?"

"Yes, sir," she replied, mimicking his level of formality.

"Then you know it's a holiday weekend, and you know that I have better things to do than be bothered with another one of your misadventures."

"Misadventures?" she asked. That hurt. "And what do you mean by *another* one? I haven't even told you what happened yet."

"Oh, I know all about what happened," Jimmy said. "You see, I was on the golf course with some buddies, getting my play time in before I have to take the family to the Winter Lantern Festival tonight."

"Isn't it too cold up there for golfing?" Laurel asked.

"I'm not done!" he shouted. Then he lowered his voice.

"No, it's not too cold when you're enjoying yourself. The course was packed. They have to do more maintenance in the winter. It tears up the turf. But anyway ..."

She waited for him to continue, glancing around to see how many people were listening. She could imagine him on a cold golf course with his friends this holiday weekend, trying his best to enjoy the game despite the weather, annoyed by any interruption. She hoped it was, at least, sunny in D.C. today.

"Okay."

"So, I'm on the golf course, and I get a call on my personal mobile phone from a Chief Tate in some tiny Tennessee town. Come to realize, that's Brad Tate ... your boyfriend. Just because we hung out socially in the past doesn't mean I want the man calling me when I'm golfing, you know?"

"Yeah."

"You can imagine my surprise when your boyfriend tells me that you were involved in a kidnapping, especially since you had not yet informed me of such. Do you have any idea how that made my blood boil?"

"Ex ..."

"What?"

"He's my ex-boyfriend. We broke up a few months ago," Laurel explained.

Jimmy paused dramatically. He'd always had a flair for the melodramatic, especially when in the middle of a rant. "Fine. Ex-boyfriend. I'll ignore the soap opera that has become your life, Dane, as long as you can explain to me why I didn't hear about this incident from you first. We have protocol for these things for a reason. I—"

"I know," Laurel conceded. "I'm sorry. I should have called you right away."

She knew it was better to be humble and take her verbal lashing than to appear disrespectful. Even though she and Jimmy got along well, there was a chain of command for a reason.

"Damn right, you should."

She closed her eyes and sighed as she thought about the events of last night. The harrowing time in the trunk, during which she'd had to keep her wits about her. The overwhelming guilt at not being able to keep her best friend's baby safe. The waiting at the police station and all the memories it brought back. Being treated like a suspect by the cocky Detective Nolan. Seeing Brad and feeling that familiar rush of warmth return to her world, only to have it turn icy cold when meeting his beautiful neighbor, Jamie. By the time Laurel had gotten home to her mom's house, she didn't have the energy for another conversation. But she couldn't explain all of that to Jimmy. It was too personal to share.

What she needed was a break.

Laurel opened her eyes to find a warm hand on her shoulder.

"JIMMY, I have to call you back," Laurel said as she pushed the button to end the call. She didn't give him a chance to object.

"Hey, there, beautiful," Brad said as he positioned himself behind the chair across from her. "Is this seat taken?"

Brad was in plainclothes, wearing a powder blue flannel shirt under his bomber jacket with dark jeans that clung in all the right places. He could have been a male model representing the picture of Tennessee sexy. Rugged and woodsy, with bright, intelligent eyes and a playful grin.

Laurel blushed. She was caught off guard. "I thought you were busy."

"I was. Now I'm here," he explained. "I thought that was Maggie's 4Runner parked out front. Is she with you?"

"No, she let me borrow her car." Laurel nodded for him to sit down.

If Brad knew she had come here to sneak a look at the scene where the infant seat was found, he didn't let on. He seemed genuinely surprised—and happy—to see her.

"You tore out of my house in a huff last night," he said softly, as he leaned toward her. "What was that all about? I wanted to call, but thought I should give you some space. You'd had a rough day."

Laurel shook her head. She still wasn't ready to talk about it. She wasn't sure how she felt. Her feelings for him were complicated. The entire situation was complicated. More so than Brad realized.

"I can't, Brad. Leave it alone. Please," she said.

Just then, Kanesha noticed Brad's presence and came over to ask if he wanted to order anything to eat or drink.

"Well, well," Kanesha said jovially to Laurel. "You didn't tell me you knew the most handsome men around. Is this big one yours?"

Laurel blushed even more, feeling like a shrinking violet. Not her usual demeanor. When she hesitated, Brad jumped in.

"Used to be. Still want to be," he said with a smile.

Kanesha's brows raised high on her forehead. "I see," she said, eyeing Laurel, who remained silent.

A quiet moment passed between the three of them. Brad grinned like a smitten fool while Laurel bit her lip so hard she thought it might pop like a tamale. When no one spoke, Kanesha returned to the task of taking Brad's order.

"I'll have whatever she's having," he said, gesturing to Laurel.

"Fisherman's Stew and a Charred Romaine Wedge?" Kanesha asked.

Brad winced. "Charred lettuce?"

"It's fancy," Kanesha said. "Or so I've been told. Don't knock it until you try it."

He shrugged. "Fine. Make it two."

"And to drink?" she asked.

Brad glanced at Laurel, then back at Kanesha.

"She's just having water," Kanesha said, before he could ask.

"I'll start with the same," he replied. "You do serve alcohol here, though, right?"

She nodded, and Brad said that he might order something later from that menu.

Kanesha seemed like she wanted to stay and chat, but the expression on Laurel's face told her she should ring the order in and make herself scarce.

Once Kanesha returned to the kitchen, Laurel couldn't hold her tongue. "Why are you acting so chummy?" she asked Brad. "Like you're pining for me?"

"What if I am? I miss you, babe. I've made no secret of the fact that I hope we get back together. I never wanted to break up in the first place. You're my one and only. I wanted to make you my wife. Remember?"

He reached across the table to take her hand. She pulled away, placing her palms in her lap, even though it practically killed her to do so. She yearned for his comforting touch.

Laurel looked at Brad intently. She wanted to say something about Jamie, but she wasn't typically the jealous type and didn't intend to appear insecure. That's never attractive. Besides, what would she say? That his tenant was too beautiful and he should rent to a crusty old man instead?

"I don't know what to say," Laurel finally replied. It was the truth.

"Say you're ready to get back to what we had," Brad implored. "I'd love nothing more."

She decided to play the scenario through with him. "What? And move back here to Appleman's Gap?"

Laurel hadn't even fully admitted it to herself, but she'd been toying with the idea. It would be nice to live near family. She could probably transfer to the Field Office in Knoxville, or one of their satellite offices in the region. If she decided to stay with the F.B.I., that was. If she left the Bureau to do something like become a private investigator, she could be based anywhere she chose.

"Ideally," Brad replied. "I'm new to the Chief job and all, trying to fill the shoes your dad left. But for you, my love, I'd follow you anywhere. You know that. Say the word, and I'll be there."

She knew he meant it. Brad had always said the same thing. That she was his world and he'd follow her anywhere. It was sweet. It was also a lot of pressure.

"I don't know," she said, taking a swig of water. "I'm not sure I'm ready to make any big decisions. I'd rather focus on the investigation, truth be told. Can you get me access? Anything new?"

Brad's expression hardened. He pursed his lips. "Actually, no," he said. "I think I convinced Nolan to get off your back, but there's no way you'll be able to participate in this investigation. You're going to have to let this one go."

"Why?" Laurel asked. "That isn't fair."

She realized she sounded like a child. Fair shouldn't have anything to do with it.

He sighed. "I have my reasons. I need you to trust me. Can you do that?"

"Should I trust that you aren't sleeping with Jamie?"

The words were out before Laurel could help herself. She

raised a hand and covered her mouth, as if to shove them back in.

Brad's face fell. "What? Why would you ask me that?"

Before she could answer, Kanesha returned with a beer and wine menu. Apparently, the woman couldn't read the room. Brad didn't mind, though.

"Two margaritas, on the rocks," he ordered, barely glancing at the options. He and Laurel had their routines. He knew what she liked.

Laurel startled. "No! I'm not drinking."

Kanesha nodded. Brad looked puzzled.

"We have a few holiday specials," Kanesha explained. "Maybe those will sound better?"

Laurel turned her head, staring out at the lake and covering her mouth again.

"Want to look at the specials, babe?" Brad asked her. "I could go for a Thanksgiving concoction. Or maybe they're on to Christmas by now. Either way."

Laurel hesitated just a moment, but in that moment, she and Brad came to an understanding as they looked deeply into each other's eyes.

"I'm not drinking," she said again.

"Just water will be fine," Brad said slowly.

And he knew. The realization sat heavy between them as Kanesha again returned to the kitchen and they were left alone.

Laurel had known for a while that she was pregnant. It was Brad's baby. She hadn't been with anyone else, and the timing was right.

She had suffered with terrible morning sickness during the first trimester, but had finally reached the point of being past that. The oppressive nausea and vomiting was one reason she hadn't been in touch with Brad. She hadn't been feeling her best, which made it more difficult to sort through her feelings.

"Are we going to talk about this?" Brad asked gently.

A smile played on his lips, and it looked like he was working hard to keep from jumping up and down right there in the crowded restaurant. He was clearly happy about the news.

It was no secret that Brad wanted to be a dad. His family and friends knew it. Even Laurel's family and friends knew it. He was a consummate nice guy who would, no doubt, be an incredible father. He was genuine in a way that not all men were. When he did something, he did it with his whole heart. Laurel was well aware that he'd be an amazing husband, too. The same way he'd been an amazing boyfriend. Her doubts weren't about him or his readiness to take the next steps. That was a no-brainer.

"I'm sorry," Laurel said, feeling suddenly emotional. Hormones had been causing her to tear up and cry more than usual.

Brad stood and moved to the chair closest to Laurel, then he sat on the edge of his seat and cupped her chin in his hand. This time, she let him touch her.

"Sorry?" he asked. "What in the world would you need to be sorry for? This is the best news of my entire life. Do you have any idea how happy this makes me?"

She nodded. "But I broke up with you. And I didn't tell you once I found out I was pregnant. And I let that man take my best friend's baby when one of my own is on the way."

She sputtered as she said the last part, tears threatening to take over.

Brad pulled her into an embrace and softly stroked her hair. "Hey, now, it will all be okay. You hear me? I'm right here. You're not alone in this anymore, okay? We'll figure things out."

Laurel pulled back, looking him in the eyes. "How is Sarah? Did you check on her?"

Brad's expression hardened again, if ever so slightly. He was holding something back. That much was evident every time Laurel mentioned Sarah or Baby Jasper, which didn't make sense. Why wouldn't he let her in on the investigation?

"She's distraught, as you'd expect. She's holding up all right, though."

"You saw her?"

He nodded. "Yes, I saw her this morning."

"Was Linda with her? I hope so. She surely needs her mom right now," Laurel said.

"Linda was there," Brad confirmed. "So was Owen."

Laurel sighed. She was glad to hear that Sarah had some support. Although she couldn't help but feel bad that Sarah had such a skeleton crew as compared to Laurel's big family. If something like this were to happen to Laurel, she'd easily have two dozen people on site to help with anything she needed. Her big family could be annoying at times, but they always showed up for each other when it counted.

Kanesha arrived with their food and placed it on the table in front of them. She gave a slight smile when she saw Laurel and Brad sitting close to each other, but she didn't comment. Laurel had developed an appetite in the time they'd been waiting. The food looked and smelled good. They dug in.

Nine

"I'M GOING TO CALL HER," Laurel said between bites of warm stew. "Well, after I call Jimmy back. I practically hung up on him when you arrived. He's probably livid by now."

Brad lowered his brows as he chewed. "Babe, please don't call Sarah. Not yet. Let things settle first."

He didn't mention Jimmy, or say why he'd placed a call to him without giving Laurel a heads up. She had plenty of questions about that, but decided to focus on one thing at a time.

Laurel put her spoon down, exasperated. "Why in the hell not? I swear, you're keeping something from me. Maybe more than one thing. What *is* it, Brad? You're making me crazy. Do you realize how impossible you're being?"

He shook his head and kept chewing. "Don't think about it like that. I'm doing what's in your best interest, while also keeping this investigation going smoothly. I promise you."

Laurel bit her tongue, even though she had so much to say. Kanesha was already watching them with great interest, probably telling other employees what a lively table she had.

Laurel hated being the center of attention. That's most likely why she felt comfortable playing horn in an orchestra rather than as a soloist. It was also mostly likely why she liked working with a team at the Bureau. Being a private investigator might prove challenging, if she had to take a more visible role, front and center.

"Does Sarah know?" Brad asked sweetly. "About our news?"

Laurel was almost mad at him for changing the subject, but she couldn't blame him for being excited about their baby.

She shook her head. "No one does. Just me, and now you."

"Oh, wow," he said. "You didn't even tell Maureen and the rest of the Dane clan?"

She shook her head again. "I wanted time to think things through. As you know, I've been considering a career change for a while now, anyway."

"Hence the extended leave," Brad said, his mouth full of stew.

He was an exuberant eater, all fast hands and quick chewing. It was remarkable that he could hold a conversation during a meal.

"Exactly," she replied.

"What are you thinking?" he asked thoughtfully.

She sighed. "I'm thinking I'd like you to treat me like a competent F.B.I. agent instead of a schoolgirl. Also that you've never kept secrets from me before, as far as I know. Why now?"

Brad shrugged, but didn't answer right away. He finished his stew, then moved on to the charred lettuce, making a perplexed face as he poured the dressing on and prepared to take the first bite.

"It's weird, isn't it?" Laurel asked with a laugh. "But seriously, Brad, talk to me."

He put the bite in his mouth and chewed, pausing only briefly before giving a thumbs up to indicate that it wasn't too bad.

"It's a small town thing," he explained. "You know how it is with families and small towns, especially when your dad was the former Chief and your boyfriend—or whatever you want to classify me as—is the current one."

Laurel wrinkled her brow. "What does that have to do with the kidnapping? Are you saying my family is somehow involved?"

"No. I mean, maybe. But not like that," he replied. "No one in your family has done anything wrong, that I know of. It's just that the connections are proving ... troublesome."

"Look," she said, "I honestly have no idea what you're talking about." She'd stopped eating, being too preoccupied with the matter at hand. "I get that there are similarities to a case my dad was investigating before he died. Right? But why is that a reason to ice me out? Do you think I can't be objective? I've literally been trained—"

"Babe, stop it," he said, taking her hand. "I have complete confidence in your abilities. It isn't that."

She held his hand, but leaned back in her chair. "Do you realize that your approach here is only making me more determined to find out what the hell is going on? I don't respond well to being told to sit back and wait. That isn't my personality. You know that."

Brad nodded as he shoveled in bites of salad with his free hand, apparently enjoying the char. "I do."

"And I was kidnapped, too. It was scary in that trunk."

That made him set his fork down and give her his full attention. He reached his other hand out and gently touched her belly. Laurel didn't pull away.

"The thought of you and our baby being in that kind of danger guts me," Brad said. "I'd lay down my life to keep the two of you safe. Badass F.B.I. agent or not, you're my world, and now I know you're carrying our baby. I could rip that asshole to shreds with my bare hands. I actually might, if I can get a hold of him."

Laurel blushed. She had to admit, she liked how protective Brad was. It reminded her of the way her dad had always treated her. She wanted the same kind of fatherly protectiveness for her own child. A pang of guilt hit her an instant later, when she thought about how Baby Jasper needed as much. Every child did.

"I'm glad you feel that way," she said, leaning her forehead against his.

It was the closest and most intimate they'd been in months. It felt like home.

Laurel closed her eyes, oblivious to the crowd around them as Brad kept one hand on hers and the other on her lower abdomen, where their precious baby was growing. The conversation was deep. She found herself caring less and less about who was watching and what they thought. She loved Brad. But she needed answers. She needed to know she could trust him.

When she opened her mouth to speak, he leaned in and almost kissed her.

She pulled back. "I'm not ready. Not yet," she said. "I have to trust—"

Before Laurel could finish her sentence, Kanesha was at the table to check on them.

"Everything okay over here? Can I get you anything else?" Kanesha asked.

Laurel and Brad said that things were good, and Kanesha seemed happy for them. Instead of walking away, though, she pulled her phone out of her back pocket and leaned down near Laurel.

"Hey, that thing you asked me about earlier?" Kanesha asked.

"Yeah?" Laurel replied, hoping that Kanesha wouldn't mention the baby seat or the investigation in front of Brad.

No such luck.

"I have a picture of the infant carrier. I thought you might want to see, since you were asking. The employee that found it in the bathroom took a picture and posted it in a group chat before our manager called it in," Kanesha explained.

She thrust the phone in Laurel's direction, allowing both Laurel and Brad to get a good look. Kanesha had no idea what a kink she had just thrown into Laurel's plans. She didn't know that Laurel and Brad were law enforcement.

Laurel's face was flush with embarrassment. She was busted. Brad would know that she was digging around on her own, even though he'd told her to steer clear of this investigation. Aside from their personal relationship and her desire to protect his feelings, Brad was Chief of Police in Appleman's Gap. Unless something had changed that Laurel wasn't aware of, he still had jurisdiction over this case.

More importantly, though, Laurel immediately recognized the seat in the picture as the one Baby Jasper had been riding in when they were kidnapped. She had buckled the baby herself, and she recognized the teal blue fabric at the top of the seat with a wavy pattern below in shades of silver.

Her stomach clenched and she felt like she might be sick. If that seat wasn't Baby Jasper's, it was *exactly* like it.

"Was that picture given to my officers?" Brad asked, his tone cool.

Kanesha's brows lifted as she leaned back, and her long braids swung. She glanced at Laurel, who simply nodded.

"He's the local Chief," Laurel said, gesturing toward Brad. "It's his investigation."

Kanesha looked confused for a moment, but then pieces of the puzzle began to come together in her mind. "Ah, I see," she said simply. She straightened. "Yes, sir, the photo was given to the officers working around back. My manager made sure of that."

Brad nodded his thanks, relaxing a bit. Laurel wondered if he would out her to Kanesha and make a scene, but he didn't. Instead, he pulled a business card and a pen out of his jacket pocket. His information was printed neatly on the front. He added Laurel's name and new mobile phone number to the back. Was this an in?

"Here," he said as he handed the card to Kanesha. "Reach out if you think of anything else we should know."

Laurel smiled, relieved that Brad had included her and hopeful that Kanesha might call.

"Ready for that box?" Kanesha asked Laurel, as if nothing had happened. "Maybe a bowl, too?"

Laurel nodded sheepishly. When Kanesha returned,

Laurel wrapped up her food to take home to her mom. Neither woman spoke another word, though Laurel made a mental note to return without Brad at some point soon and set the record straight.

PART TWO

Family Drama

Ten

THE REST of the day passed in a haze. Laurel lounged on the sofa at her mom's house, watching mindless TV with various family members who trickled in and out.

All five Dane siblings had been at Maureen's for Thanksgiving dinner, and Cornelius' absence had hung heavy in the air. It was the first big family holiday without him. His empty chair at the table was a painful reminder of how much they'd lost, yet no one had the nerve to sit there in his place. Not even Mikey, Maureen and Cornelius' oldest son, who fancied himself the new man of the house. They weren't that kind of family, anyway, but it would be hard to act as man of the house from all the way over in Knoxville. Mikey, his wife, Jessica, and their three young children would soon head back east to be at school and work on Monday morning. Mikey and his family were settled in Knoxville, and Laurel doubted they'd ever move to Appleman's Gap.

Laurel hadn't called Jimmy, but she'd texted, somehow convincing him that finishing their discussion could wait until another day. He had all the information he needed from

Brad, she figured. She resented Jimmy and Brad's social connections and was mad that they both seemed to be coddling her. She'd need to figure out how to handle them.

Laurel was seriously bummed. She felt like a caged animal, with nowhere to go. She couldn't pursue the kidnapping investigation without stumbling into whatever weird family dynamics Brad had spoken of. She couldn't contact Sarah, either. And she wasn't sure how she felt about Brad now knowing about their baby. Until Laurel could come up with a solid plan for where to turn next, she intended to veg out.

As the hours wore on, Laurel fell asleep. She'd found herself doing a lot of that lately. It was early the next morning before the sounds of Maureen moving around in the kitchen woke her. Well, that and her insistent bladder. Pregnancy hormones kept her in the bathroom far more often these days.

She shook her head to clear it as she hoisted herself off the sofa and made her way to the toilet. She absentmindedly raised a hand to her belly as she walked past the kitchen, causing her mom to do a double take.

"What?" Laurel asked, without slowing down. "Mom, you'll catch flies if you keep your mouth hanging open like that."

Maureen might have a hint about her bun in the oven, but she'd have to wait until after Laurel relieved herself to discuss it.

Laurel knew that it was only a matter of time before she had to tell everyone her little secret. She was beginning to show. Her growing bump could still be hidden with baggy winter clothes and a coat, but anything else was becoming too revealing.

She finished quickly in the powder room, knowing that she needed to get into the full bathroom and shower soon. Thanks to military training, Laurel always felt better when she got up and dressed early in the day. She had limited tolerance for lounging around in pajamas, and she'd already done enough of that. She splashed some cold water on her face, then went to chat with her mom.

When she found her mom in the kitchen, Maureen's eyes were wet with tears.

"Mom, what is it?" Laurel asked, sliding an arm around Maureen's delicate shoulders. "Don't cry."

Maureen closed her eyes and shook her head. "Child, don't tell me what to do. You don't know my sorrows."

She was serious, which struck Laurel as strange. Maybe she was becoming paranoid, but it almost seemed like there was something important that Maureen wasn't telling her.

"Are you sad about Dad?" Laurel asked. "It was terrible to celebrate Thanksgiving without him. I know I feel guilty about life going on when he's not here. Maybe you do, too?"

Maureen's tears came faster, her voice catching as she tried to speak. "He was my world, Laurel. For longer than you've been alive. Cornelius Dane was my everything. All I really cared about was being with him. I would have followed him anywhere. Done anything to be with him. Anything to spend a few more minutes by his side, with his big, strong hand on mine. Do you have any idea how a love like that feels?"

Laurel did know. She felt that way about Brad, but she'd gone and ruined their relationship by breaking up with him. She didn't think her mom could ever understand why she'd done such a thing, so she kept quiet about it.

"I'm sorry, Mom," she said. "I know you loved him so much."

Maureen grabbed a tissue from a box in the pantry, then dried her face as best she could. "I guess I didn't expect to get this kind of news today. It hits different without him here by my side. If I had my druthers, your dad would be right here with me."

"What news?" Laurel asked innocently, knowing full well what her mom was referring to.

Maureen ignored that and kept right on moving. "Does Brad know?"

At least, Maureen wasn't asking if it was Brad's baby. She knew he was Laurel's one and only love. Laurel took it as a vote of confidence that her mom didn't suspect her of sleeping around after she'd broken up with Brad.

She hadn't. She wouldn't.

"Know what?" Laurel tried. It was a feeble attempt at avoiding the subject, but it was worth a shot.

Maureen lowered one brow, looking skeptical. "Really?"

Before Laurel could fess up, Mikey strolled into the kitchen, his hair disheveled from sleep and a terry cloth robe tied tightly around his trim waist. Since everyone else already lived in Appleman's Gap, Laurel and Mikey were the only siblings staying at Maureen's while in town. Mikey could tell that he'd walked in on something juicy, and he was delighted by the chance to hear some good gossip.

"What's up, sis?" he asked Laurel as he opened the door to the refrigerator and peered inside. "You working on a case?"

Laurel wished it were that simple. "I'd love to be working on the kidnapping case, but the local cronies have pushed me right out," she replied. "I honestly have no idea why they're staying so tight-lipped. Especially since I was the one kidnapped, too. It doesn't make sense."

Maureen shot her a look, which she strategically ignored.

"Need me to hack into something for you?" Mikey asked, only half joking.

Maggie might have been able to point Laurel to an online police scanner, but their brother's skills were significantly more advanced.

Mikey was a cybersecurity analyst who worked for the Department of Defense from his home overlooking the Tennessee River. He traveled to D.C. for meetings sometimes, and he and Laurel would hang out together when he did. Most of the time, though, he did his work from his home office in Knoxville. Being a huge introvert, he liked it that way.

Laurel laughed. "See, I've always suspected you were part of some hacktivist group like Anonymous. I'm right, aren't I?"

Mikey smiled, pulling a jug of milk out of the fridge and filling a glass. "Anonymous members are by very definition ... *anonymous*. If I was one of them, I could never tell."

Laurel and Maureen laughed, although Laurel was pretty sure that her mom had no idea what they were talking about.

"Hey, isn't Brad one of those local cronies now?" Mike asked, shoving a hand through his wavy blonde hair.

He knew Brad even better than the rest of the family, thanks to the extra time they'd spent together during Mikey's trips to D.C. In fact, Mikey and Brad were friends. Laurel was a bit surprised that they hadn't kept in touch. *If* they hadn't kept in touch.

"You two haven't talked?" Laurel asked her brother.

Mikey shook his head. "No, sis. My loyalty lies with you. You know that."

Laurel blushed, thinking about how, one way or another, Brad would remain a part of their lives, now that she was carrying his baby. She guessed it was good that Brad and her brother had been friends. She hoped the family wouldn't be too hard on her baby daddy, although she practically shuddered to think of him in those terms. Brad Tate was so much more to her.

"Aww, thanks, Mikey," Laurel said, walking to where her brother was standing and giving his shoulder a nudge. "You're a good brother, you know?"

Mikey chuckled, but he could tell that something deeper was going on. "Sis, are you okay? Tell me the truth."

Laurel's face fell. She was so frustrated by the feeling that people weren't telling her the truth. The last thing she wanted to do was hoist that feeling onto her loved ones. Truth was becoming more and more important to her, by the minute.

Should she confide in Mikey? She'd like to open up to someone, that was for sure.

Sensing the siblings' desire for privacy, Maureen excused herself. "Well, that about puts the rag on the bush," she said. "I'll leave you two to discuss whatever it is that's on your mind." She eyed Laurel as she left the room, letting her know that they'd need to continue the baby conversation later.

Once they were alone, Mikey took a seat at a barstool and Laurel settled next to him. They picked at a plate of fruit and croissants absentmindedly. Both were preoccupied. When Mikey finally spoke, his tone was gentle.

"Tell me," he said.

Laurel sighed, dropping the act. She wouldn't try to pretend that everything was fine. She needed a friend, and Mikey was a good one.

"Go on," he urged. "Let it out."

At that, Laurel burst into tears. She'd been so strong for so long. She knew it wasn't good for an F.B.I. agent to devolve into a blubbering mess. Such a display would diminish her credibility, if the guys at the Bureau saw. The same would be true for any law enforcement setting. Agents weren't supposed to get emotional. But this was personal time, and Mikey was her brother. He reached out and put an arm around her, pulling her to him.

"Sorry," she mumbled.

"Oh, hush," he said. "Even superhero big sisters need a good cry sometimes."

She laughed, then cried some more. "Is that how you think of me?" she finally asked, pulling back. "As a superhero."

He nodded quickly. "Ever since you wore that Wonder Woman costume for Halloween. What were you, in about fifth grade?"

"Something like that."

"You were a vision. It's like it all clicked for me. I saw you the way you truly are," Mikey explained.

Eleven

LAUREL AND MIKEY spent a few more minutes reminiscing about their sibling relationship and childhood, but Mikey's kids soon woke up and stormed the kitchen. Sensing that she needed some quiet time to share her burdens, Mikey invited his sister to lunch.

"Do you have time?" Laurel asked. "I know you're heading back to Knoxville today."

"Of course, I do," Mikey replied. "Jess won't mind keeping the kids occupied for a while."

"You sure?"

"One hundred percent."

Relieved, Laurel agreed to the outing, then she got herself showered and dressed. By the time she returned to the main living area of Maureen's house, Mikey was already there waiting on her. They grabbed their coats and hurried out the door. It had been a long time since they'd gone out, just the two of them. As the next youngest sibling after Laurel, Mikey held a special place in his sister's heart.

"I take it you're riding with me," Mikey said with a

chuckle as he unlocked the door to his family's white mini-van. He had a Jeep at home, but traveling with three young children meant that he needed more space. The van was one of those new, sporty models with angular sides and plenty of convenience features. It almost didn't feel like you were riding in a minivan.

"Yep," Laurel said. "Still no word on my car. I guess I should get a rental, if it doesn't show up in the next day or two. I can't sit around Mom's house all the time. I'll go insane. Maggie let me borrow her 4Runner yesterday, but I don't want to be a bother. You know how she gets when her independence is infringed on."

"Do you blame her?" Mikey asked.

Laurel shook her head as she climbed into the passenger seat and buckled her seatbelt. "No, I don't."

Satisfied, Mikey moved on to more pressing matters. "Where to?"

Laurel thought for a moment. There were plenty of great restaurants in Appleman's Gap. In fact, the area was lucky to have quite the foodie scene for a small town. She had a hunch, though, that she should go back to see her friend Kanesha. Without Brad there, she could ask more questions. It had seemed like Kanesha wanted to say more.

"How about Jack and Jill's?" Laurel asked.

"Weren't you just there yesterday?"

"I was. There's a friendly server who shared a picture of the baby seat found in their bathroom. I suspect she might tell me more, given the opportunity."

"Ah, I see," Mikey said, a knowing look settling on his face. "So, this is the unofficial investigation that you aren't supposed to be doing."

"Maybe," Laurel replied with a smile. "You're okay with that, aren't you?"

"One hundred percent."

They chatted as they made the short drive to Hillside Marina. It was another sunny day for late November, and Jack and Jill's was busy. As soon as Laurel stepped out of the van and smelled the water, she could feel herself relax. They had to wait a few minutes for a table, but they didn't mind one bit. The restaurant provided big heaters in the waiting area just like the ones in the dining room. Sitting there and watching the water lap at the rocks was no problem at all. Quite the contrary. It was a treat.

"Who do we ask for?" Mikey asked.

"Already done," Laurel replied. "Kanesha. When I put our name in, I asked that we be seated in her section."

Mikey nodded. "Got it. Anything else I should know before I meet her?"

Laurel shrugged. "Just that Brad showed up when I was here yesterday fishing for information. He didn't intend to, but he kind of made me look like an ass."

"Oh? How so?"

"Well, when Kanesha mentioned the baby seat, Brad got all stuffy and announced his official title. It could have been worse, I suppose. I was afraid he was going to say something about me staying away from the investigation. He stopped short of that."

Mikey nodded again. "Hey, I'm on your side, sis, but it sounds like Brad has a lot of balls in the air. You know?"

Laurel grimaced. "Poor, pitiful Brad."

"Come on, now," Mikey said. "I'm simply saying that he must have someone telling him to keep you away. Because I don't think he'd make that decision on his own. I've always known Brad to be enamored with you and in awe of your professional abilities. He told me many times how he hoped to be half as good as you were, but that he knew he'd never measure up."

"I guess I hadn't thought about it that way," she replied. "You think someone is on his back?"

"I do."

"But who? As far as I know, he still has jurisdiction over this case. I'm not aware of anything that would change that. Not yet."

"I don't know," Mikey said. "But we can probably find out."

Laurel nodded, deep in thought. Before she could say anything else, her phone buzzed with a text message saying that their table was ready. They made their way to the hostess stand, then followed the young woman to a table and settled into seats across from each other. Today's table was even closer to the water than yesterday's. Laurel relished the serene view.

WIthin minutes, Kanesha arrived to take their drink order, clearly surprised to see Laurel again. "Well, well, well," she began. "What brings you back here so soon?" She looked skeptically at Mikey, clearly unsure what to make of him.

Laurel decided that, this time, she'd put everything outfront from the very beginning. "This is my brother, Mikey," she said. "Mikey, meet Kanesha."

"The pleasure is all mine," Kanesha said, seeming to take a shine to Laurel's brother. Laurel started to get concerned, but then saw Kanesha notice his wedding band.

Mikey was happy in his marriage to Jessica. The last thing

Laurel wanted was to stir up trouble for him in that department. It was really nothing to be concerned about, though. Even if an attractive woman like Kanesha came on to Mikey, he wouldn't respond to her advances. His marriage was rock solid. Laurel hoped that she'd have a relationship like that someday. Granted, she *did* have a relationship like that with Brad, yet she'd gone and screwed it up. She could have kicked herself.

"Drinks?" Kanesha asked. "Water for you, Laurel?"

She remembered Laurel's name. That much was good. Mentioning water wasn't great, but Laurel intended to tell Mikey about the pregnancy. So, it was fine.

"Yes," Laurel replied.

Mikey ordered water, too, and didn't seem phased by the fact that his sister wasn't ordering alcohol. It wasn't like she drank all the time, anyway,

Once Kanesha left the table, Laurel jumped right in. She wanted to make the most of the time they had together.

"Before we get into anything else, I have something personal to tell you," Laurel said. She felt a little nervous, like a kid confessing an embarrassing secret. Although, she wasn't sure why. She was a grown woman who had been in a committed, loving relationship. Her child was conceived out of love.

"Okay. What?" Mikey asked.

Laurel didn't hesitate. She decided to rip the band-aid off. "I'm pregnant."

"Congratulations," he said, not the slightest bit surprised.

Laurel was confused. "Wait. You knew?"

Mikey laughed. "Don't be mad, but yeah."

"How?"

"Sis, I have three kids. I know a little something about pregnant women," he explained.

"Is it that obvious?"

He shrugged. "Your boobs are bigger, you have that glow everyone talks about, and honestly, at this point, you're showing. Don't try to tell me that bump is just a few too many helpings of Mom's sweet potato casserole at Thanksgiving."

Laurel instinctively placed a hand over her lower abdomen.

If Mikey and Maureen could both tell, then lots of other people could, too. Laurel would need to start making announcements, if she wanted to stay ahead of the rumor mill. Gossip had a way of spreading quickly in small towns like Appleman's Gap. Not to mention, she and Brad needed to get on the same page and form a united front. That might be easier said than done, with Jamie in the picture.

"But thanks for telling me," Mikey said. "I take it I'm one of the first to know?"

She nodded. "The second. I told Brad yesterday. Although, Mom seemed to know this morning. I didn't confirm her suspicions, though. You interrupted us. Great timing, dear brother."

"Telling Mom won't be so bad. She loves her grandkids to pieces."

"Yeah."

"I guess our friend Brad will be sticking around, after all," Mikey said with a smile. "I can't say that I'm too bummed about that. He'll be a great father."

Laurel couldn't help but smile at that. "I guess it takes one to know one."

Mikey truly was a wonderful father. He was a great son,

brother, husband, and friend, too, but the role of father was where he really shone the brightest. Cornelius had been the same, which must have been where Mikey learned his parenting skills.

Kanesha arrived with their glasses of water, then proceeded to rattle off the daily specials. She didn't seem to realize she'd walked up on a weighty conversation. It was fine.

"No Fisherman's Stew today?" Laurel asked.

"Nope. Out of it," Kanesha replied.

"That's okay. I'm hungrier this time. No one made me a sandwich out of leftovers at home this morning," Laurel said.

Mikey ordered a burger and a side salad while Laurel pored over the menu, studying it carefully. Finally, she ordered fish tacos with a salad of her own. She was tempted to get fries, but didn't want to let pregnancy weight gain spiral out of control. She hoped to feel like some semblance of her old self again once this baby was born.

Before Kanesha left to ring in their order, Laurel put a hand on her forearm and motioned for her to lean towards them. "Hey, I want you to know that you can speak freely today. If you know anything else about that baby seat, I encourage you to tell me."

Kanesha nodded, glancing at Mikey.

"I'm not law enforcement," Mikey said. "I promise. I'm no threat. I work on a computer from my home office and don't talk to anyone but Bogart, the family cat. Say anything you want to around me."

Laurel doubled down. "I didn't mention it yesterday, Kanesha, but I'm an agent with the Federal Bureau of Investigation. I'm here on leave and not officially working this case, but I can assure you that anything you tell me will be handled with the utmost care and discretion. I just want to find that baby and bring him home safely."

Kanesha nodded. "I thought you were something. I didn't know what. But something. And your man from yesterday? The new Chief?"

Kanesha hadn't articulated a specific question, but Laurel knew what she meant.

"He's a good guy," Laurel said, and Mikey confirmed with a nod. "He might be a little overzealous in trying to protect me. We were together for six years."

"You sure looked together," Kanesha said with a chuckle.

Laurel smiled. "I know. There's still a lot of love between us. We'll figure it out."

Kanesha paused, a realization seeming to dawn on her. "Protect you from what? Are you the woman who was kidnapped along with that baby?"

Mikey raised his brows. "She's a smart one," he mused.

Laurel knew there was no point in trying to hide it. "Yes, that's right. It was my car. I was tossed into the trunk. The baby belongs to my closest friend, which is why I want so badly to help find him and bring him home safely."

Kanesha nodded quickly. "Stay here. I'll be right back."

She scurried off, stopping at the register to put their orders in, then she disappeared into the kitchen.

"What do you think that's about?" Mikey asked.

"I don't know," Laurel said. "But I hope she has something useful for me."

He agreed. They both stared out at the water, enjoying each other's company. They were also deep in thought about the kidnapping, the pregnancy, and how Brad would figure in.

"Are you going to get back together?" Mikey asked, after a moment.

"Too soon to tell," Laurel said, although she knew deep down that was a lie. She belonged in Brad's life. In his arms. She just had to be sure she could trust him again. And she had to get her own mind settled about Jamie. Laurel would have loved to see Jamie disappear from Appleman's Gap altogether.

Couldn't someone offer Jamie a job transfer or something? Anything to get her out of here.

"Okay, sure," Mikey replied. "Let me rephrase that. What needs to happen for you and Brad to get back together and live happily ever after with the baby the two of you created?"

Laurel shrugged. "He's hiding something. I need to know what."

Twelve

BY THE TIME Kanesha returned to their table, she had their food with her. Everything looked and smelled delicious. Almost delicious enough to make Laurel forget about whatever it was that Kanesha wanted to show her. She blamed pregnancy hormones.

"Thanks," Laurel said.

"Don't you worry," Kanesha added. "I'm working on something that might help you find that baby. I'll have it ready before you leave. You have my word."

Laurel nodded, then took a big bite of a taco. Mikey chuckled. He obviously recognized his sister's ravenous appetite and got a kick out of it.

"Glad I invited you to lunch," he said as Kanesha walked away. "You really are eating for two."

Laurel made a face, but didn't stop chewing long enough to vocalize an answer.

Mikey was a much gentler eater than Brad. He took slow, deliberate bites, careful not to make a mess of things.

"A penny for your thoughts?" Mikey asked when he noticed his sister looking at him.

Laurel shrugged. "Just thinking about Brad and what an enthusiastic eater he is. I wonder if our baby will be like him in that regard."

Mikey laughed. "If he—or she—is lucky."

They both took a few more bites, enjoying the reprieve from serious talk. There was much to discuss, though, and Mikey wanted to do what he could to help.

"Hey," Mikey said. "What can I do for you?"

"Tech wise?" Laurel asked.

"Tech or otherwise. What do you need?"

She shrugged again, still chewing. She was making short work of the tacos. "I don't suppose you can hack into police computers and find out what the hell is going on with the investigation?"

"Would that help?" Mikey asked. He didn't say no.

"I don't want you to do anything unethical," she replied. "Especially not on my account. If you got in trouble, I'd never forgive myself. Your family needs you."

"Okay, then what? What's next?"

Laurel pushed her plate away, finally full to the brim. She felt so much better. She took a big drink of water as she thought.

"I don't know," she said. "Maybe I just need a break in the case that will point me in the right direction. It seems like my hands are tied, at the moment. I need more to go on."

"Do you think your friend Kanesha has something useful?"

"Maybe," Laurel replied. "She's clearly bright. And she

showed me a picture of the baby seat yesterday. If she thinks she has something, she probably does."

Right on cue, Kanesha arrived. She was holding a brown paper bag with tissue paper stuffed inside. A Jack and Jill's logo was stamped onto the bag in brilliant blue ink.

"What's this?" Laurel asked as Kanesha handed her the bag. For a moment, she thought maybe Kanesha had brought her a baby gift.

Kanesha leaned close and talked quietly. "There are cameras all over the place, so I had to disguise what I'm giving you. Officially, it's a Jack and Jill's t-shirt, size medium. Hope it fits. Inside, though, is a baby's teething ring. One of the cooks bought a new car yesterday and said he found the teething ring under a seat. It might be nothing, but I thought I should get it to you, just in case."

Laurel stiffened, her senses suddenly on high alert. She began to hear Mozart's Requiem in D Minor in the background. Hearing classical music in her mind was something that happened when she was onto an important clue in a case. Like a hunch or an instinct, it didn't happen all the time, but when it did, Laurel could count on the fact that there was a truth to be revealed. It was a sure sign that she should take notice.

She reached out and took Kanesha's hand in hers. "What kind of car did he buy?"

"I'm not sure," Kanesha replied.

"Is he here? Can I ask him myself?"

Now it was Mikey's turn to stiffen. He seemed uncomfortable, like he didn't want Laurel to make a scene. Or get herself into trouble, was more like it. He didn't comment, though.

Kanesha stood straight and set the bag down on the table. "Maybe I can say you wanted to speak to one of the cooks about allergens. That might do the trick without getting anyone's feathers ruffled. Let me see what I can do."

She nodded, then headed back to the kitchen.

Mikey finished his food, just in time to push his plate aside, lean his elbows on the table, and question his sister. "What's happening, Sis? I recognize that look on your face. You're hearing the music, aren't you?"

Laurel nodded. She had no desire to lie to Mikey. Not now, and not ever. He was one of her closest confidants. She had a feeling she was going to need his help. "Mozart's Requiem," she confirmed.

Mikey knew about Laurel's hunches and how they were always right. He knew what it meant when she was cued in like that. "What are you going to do with the teething ring?" he asked.

"I need to have a forensic analysis performed on it, in case there's DNA evidence. We need to confirm that it belongs to Baby Jasper. But also, the perp might have touched it. That could, potentially, lead us right to him."

"How are you going to accomplish that without involving Brad?" Mikey asked. "Doesn't seem possible. Unless you somehow get Jimmy to cooperate with sending it to an F.B.I. lab. Is the F.B.I. involved?"

Laurel shook her head. "Not as far as I know. If I had even a cursory reason to get them involved, believe me, I would. I know so many people at the Bureau who owe me favors."

"So, what? Do we need to find a private lab?"

Laurel lowered her brow. That wasn't a bad idea. If she ended up becoming a private investigator and staying in

Tennessee, she'd need a relationship with a private lab. "Maybe," she replied. "I wonder how fast they could move. We need to find that baby. No matter how much I might want to be involved, I won't allow progress to be slowed. Brad might be the more expeditious route."

Mikey nodded his agreement.

In what felt like no time at all, Kanesha was back, a sheepish young man in a white apron trailing behind her. The music continued to play in Laurel's head. It seemed to intensify in both speed and volume as the man approached.

"This is it," Laurel said to her brother, bumping his arm.

Kanesha looked pleased. "Ma'am," she said to Laurel, pretending she was any other customer. "This is one of our cooks, Dale Morgan. I told him you'd like to speak with him."

Dale stepped forward, looking nervous. He was the stereotypical country boy. Laurel imagined that he'd probably been fishing recently, even though it was cold outside, and that he probably referred to the area where he lived as a "holler."

"What can I do for you, ma'am?" Dale asked, his voice syrupy sweet. It wasn't an act, though. This was him.

Laurel got right to it. "Yes, actually, I heard that you bought a new car yesterday. Can you tell me what kind and color?"

He looked at his feet, shifting his weight from one to the other. "It was a red Honda. What do you need to know for?"

Music surged in Laurel's mind, as if a conductor had asked the orchestra to crescendo. She could almost feel the beat pulsing through her body, just like when she'd played horn.

Her car was a red Honda Accord. This couldn't possibly be a coincidence.

"Does it have black alloy wheels?" she asked.

"Yes."

"Show me," Laurel said, leaping to her feet.

"Now?" Dale asked. "I'm on shift for two more hours."

Laurel paid little attention, instead heading for the parking lot. "Is it out front?"

Dale followed after her, having to break into a jog to keep up. Mikey threw some cash down on the table to cover the bill, then he and Kanesha joined the procession out the front door.

When Laurel reached the parking lot, she put a hand above her eyes to block the sun, then she quickly scanned the surrounding area. It took less than a minute to spot it.

"There!" she said, moving quickly in the direction of the vehicle. *Her* vehicle.

Dale caught up just as Laurel bent down to look inside. He was out of breath, which was strange at his young age. He smelled like cigarette smoke, though. He didn't look like a man in the best of health.

"Lady, are you crazy?" Dale puffed.

"Not at all. This is my car."

"This ain't yours," Dale said. "I bought it, fair and square."

Laurel sighed. She knew where Dale was coming from. This must be terribly frustrating for him. To be positive, she checked the VIN number displayed on the dash. Sure enough, the number matched. Given the circumstances, there wasn't any option other than to call Brad and get his team on this.

Laurel glanced at Mikey, who had grabbed her handbag on the way out of the restaurant. He was holding it awkwardly in one hand, its strap dangling almost to the pavement.

"Hand me my bag, please," she said to her brother as Dale continued to look on in disbelief. When she took the bag, she fished around for a moment until she found the credentials that identified her as an F.B.I. agent. She showed them to Dale, his eyes going even wider.

"Whoa," he said.

Kanesha smiled, seeming pleased with Laurel's find. She had played an important role, after all. She ought to be proud.

"Sir," Laurel said to Dale, "This car was stolen and was used in a crime. It's possible there's evidence inside that would lead law enforcement to a dangerous criminal. Now, if you didn't have anything to do with that crime, you don't need to worry. You can give your statement to the police. However, I'm confiscating this vehicle immediately. Stay put."

Dale looked as if he might thrash around like an angry teenager, but he maintained his composure while Laurel pulled out her phone and dialed Brad. The new Chief answered on the first ring.

"Hey, babe," Brad said casually. He, apparently, thought this was a social call. "What's up?"

Laurel's voice was cool and business-like. It was time for Agent Dane to reappear.

"I need you to come to Jack and Jill's right away. I'm here with a stolen vehicle that's confirmed via VIN number to be the one involved in the kidnapping that took place on Friday evening. A witness says he bought the car yesterday and that he found an infant teething ring under a seat. I'm in posses-sion of both."

Brad didn't mince words, and he didn't argue Laurel's right to be involved. He simply stated, in his serious voice, "I'm on my way."

Thirteen

BEFORE THEY KNEW IT, Jack and Jill's was swarming with police cars. So many that Laurel was surprised they had this kind of presence in Appleman's Gap. Had they expanded the force since Brad took over?

Mikey was thinking the same thing. "Boy, Brad's really beefing up our little town's police presence, isn't he?"

Laurel smiled. "Speak of the devil," she said as Brad's truck rolled up. She had to admit, she was glad to see him.

"Right on time," Mikey said.

He parked quickly and hopped out, keeping the engine running. A little black nose appeared against the passenger side window. "Aww, he has Lilly with him," Laurel said, momentarily dropping her Agent Dane role.

"I take it Lilly is his dog?" Mikey asked. "If she's a new girlfriend, she's awfully short. And hairy."

Laurel punched her brother in the arm. "Hush," she said playfully.

Then she cleared her throat and got back to the task at hand. Even though she wanted to reach out for Brad when he stood next to her smelling all woodsy and looking handsome in a flannel shirt and jeans that—just like the ones he was wearing the day before—clung in all the right places, she kept a straight, serious face. His familiar bomber jacket was in his hands. He quickly slung it over his shoulders and slid his arms inside. It was Sunday, and he had probably been at home when she called.

"Why aren't you wearing a coat?" he asked Laurel, a look of genuine concern on his face. "It's freezing out here."

Mikey had grabbed her coat from the restaurant, too, and was holding it at the ready. "Slow down, boss," Mikey said to Brad. "Her coat is right here. I'm watching out for her."

Laurel bristled. She liked that Brad and Mikey were protective of her, but she didn't like them talking about it in front of Dale and Kanesha. It undermined her role as an Agent.

"I'm fine," Laurel said, shrugging on her coat as Mikey guided it behind her. She'd been too fired up over the car and the teething ring to feel the cold. "Can we get down to business?"

Brad reluctantly agreed, seeming like it was hard for him to resist taking her into his arms. After a pause to squeeze Laurel's arm and give Mikey a fist bump, Brad pursed his lips. "What do we have?" he asked.

Laurel proceeded to go over the details as she understood them, offering more than she had over the phone. She knew they'd all need to head to the station to give statements while a team processed the scene. Once Brad had arranged a ride for Dale with one of his officers, Mikey and Laurel climbed into the minivan and headed downtown. Kanesha followed in her own car, seeming excited to take part.

The late November sun was still shining when they arrived at the police station. Snow on the ground was beginning to melt, but white patches still lined the property. This time, Brad leashed Lilly and got her out of the truck. Laurel smiled, hoping for a chance to snuggle the pup. She felt badly about how short she'd been when she met Lilly on Friday night. It wasn't the dog's fault that Jamie's presence had put Laurel into a funk.

"I see you eyeing that dog," Mikey said with a chuckle. "You haven't met her yet?"

"Briefly, the other night," she replied. "I was too upset about the blonde woman living in Brad's carriage house to pay her the proper attention, though."

"Oh, that," Mikey said.

"You knew?"

"There's not much to know, Sis. I'd leave it alone, if I were you."

Laurel was irritated, but there wasn't time to get into this conversation. She waved her brother off. They'd revisit the subject later. "Let's go inside. This is the first big break in the case. We want to move fast in case it helps us find Baby Jasper. Every minute counts."

"Of course. There will be plenty of time to convince you to get back together with Brad. Later," Mikey said with a smile as they watched Kanesha and Dale enter the building.

"Again, hush," Laurel said as she got out and made her way inside. She paused at the front door and shot a text to Jimmy. Mikey waited beside her.

> Break in the case. Located my stolen car.
> A guy who says he bought it yesterday
> found an infant teething ring under the
> seat. Turned it all over to Brad. His team is
> processing now. Will keep you updated.

The phone made a whooshing sound as the text was sent.

"There," Laurel said. "I informed him."

"Who's that?" Brad asked as he arrived at the door with Lilly. He'd let the pup relieve herself in some grass around the side of the building.

"Jimmy," Laurel said, then she crouched down to give the pup's ears a scratch.

Brad nodded. "Okay."

As much as Mikey enjoyed seeing Brad and his sister chat, he wanted to get inside and get this over with. He was supposed to drive his family back to Knoxville today. The kids would need to get in bed so they'd be rested for school tomorrow.

"Hey, I don't want to rush things, but I'm heading home today," he said. "Should I tell Jess to go ahead without me? If so, that's not a problem, but she'll need the van."

Brad opened the door and gestured for them to walk inside. "Let's talk, Mikey, then you can make whatever arrangements you think best."

They walked in the door and past the reception desk. Construction paper turkeys in autumn colors made from kid-size handprints were taped to the front. Laurel hadn't noticed them on Friday night. She chalked it up to having been traumatized. Who wouldn't have been, at that point?

Matt wasn't in his chair behind the desk, and Laurel was a

little disappointed. "Where's my friend, Officer Wilson?" she asked.

"He doesn't work on weekends," Brad said, matter of factly. "Let's go to my office. All the way down the hall and—"

"Yeah, you mean our dad's office?" Laurel asked. She hadn't intended to sound snippy, but she heard it come out that way.

Mikey just shook his head. "What she means is that we grew up visiting this police station. We know our way around. You understand."

"I do," Brad replied as he unlocked his office door, flipped on the light, and motioned for them to file in.

Brad detached Lilly's leash, then she trotted happily to a soft dog bed on the floor underneath his desk. She'd obviously been here before. Laurel was happy to see Brad and Lilly together. Brad needed a companion to keep him company.

They all took seats, and Brad pulled a manilla file folder out from a drawer. He placed it on the desk in front of him, then rested both palms on top.

"What do you have there?" Laurel asked.

Brad smiled sympathetically. "How about we begin with some good news?"

Mikey gave a thumbs up, so Brad continued.

"We found Bear. He's shaken up, but okay."

"Oh, thank God," Laurel said, glancing at Lilly. She had a soft spot for family pets, particularly dogs and cats. She'd been sick over the thought of Sarah missing her canine companion and her son at the same time.

Mikey looked confused. It took a moment, but then it dawned on him. "Oh, the dog. Right!"

"Sarah's dog," Laurel clarified. She put a hand over her heart. "That really is such good news. How did you find him?"

"A deputy was searching the industrial area near where he ran away this morning," Brad explained. "Our guys had been there several times before, but this particular deputy brought some of his aunt's Thanksgiving gravy as a bargaining chip. The gravy was warm, and he knew Bear would be hungry. All it took was a heaping spoonful of the good stuff on top of some kibble and Bear emerged from the shadows to partake."

"Nice," Mikey said. "Never underestimate the power of a warm meal. None of us could resist."

Brad chuckled, but Laurel and Mikey could tell that there was bad news coming. He had more to say.

"Is he home with Sarah?" Laurel asked.

"He is. Sarah and Linda were very happy to see him. I dropped him off less than an hour ago. In fact, I brought Lilly along to help Bear feel more comfortable. I think it worked, because he leaned against her in my truck as I drove. I took a picture. Here, let me show you."

Brad pulled out his phone and enlarged the photo. Both dogs looked happy as clams.

"That's great, Brad," Laurel said sincerely. "What's the bad news?"

He didn't bother arguing with her. She knew him too well for that. Instead, he leaned back in his chair and crossed his hands behind his head. He took a deep breath, steeling himself for what came next.

"I'm glad Mikey's here with you," Brad said to Laurel. His tone was soft. It was the voice of Brad who loved her and wanted the best for her, not Brad the Chief of Police.

Mikey reached over and took Laurel's hand in his. "We've got her," he said. "We've got them both."

The men exchanged a knowing glance, and Mikey didn't need to go any further in discussing the baby.

Brad paused. It seemed like he really didn't want to say whatever it was he had to.

"Brad, get it over with," Laurel said. "I know you've been hiding things from me. I'd feel better knowing the truth."

"I'm not so sure about that," Brad replied. He shook his head, sadly.

A silence stretched between them until, finally, Brad mustered the courage to speak. "There's been a ransom request."

"For Baby Jasper?" Laurel asked. "Is he safe?"

"Yes. He's alive, for now."

"Thank God and the heavens," Laurel said, tears springing to her eyes.

Mikey held up a finger, sensing that it wasn't that simple. "And?" he asked.

"And ... the ransom money has to come from Maureen."

Laurel and Mikey both slid forward in their seats, shock evident on their faces.

"As in, our mom, Maureen?" Mikey asked.

Brad nodded. "I didn't want to tell any of you until I was sure it wasn't some jokester orchestrating an elaborate prank. The leader of the kidnapping syndicate calls himself The Cradler, which struck me as theatrical. That name sounds like it's fit for a comic book villain. Unfortunately, this villain is very real. I've had a crime lab in Nashville working around the clock. DNA results came back while I was at Sarah's, returning Bear."

"DNA? I'm confused," Laurel said. "Do you think our mom was involved with the kidnapping? Because there's no way—"

"Of course not," Brad replied as Mikey and Laurel held tightly to each other.

"Then what?" Mikey asked.

Brad sighed. "The kidnappers who have Baby Jasper claim that he's Cornelius' grandson. We tested DNA comparing a sample on file for your dad and some strands of hair from the baby's brush. Tests confirm that the kidnappers are right."

"That's bullshit," Mikey blurted, his demeanor uncharacteristically angry. "Someone made a mistake. Run the test again."

"We did. Three times," Brad said. "Look, I felt the same way. I'm protective of your dad. I thought the claim would turn out to be bogus. I'm just as surprised as you are."

"Is that even legal?" Mikey asked. "To test a dead man's DNA? Did Mom give you permission?"

"She didn't need to," Brad replied. "Cornelius already had. He was actually the one who instituted a policy where all personnel are required to submit a DNA sample to be kept on file. I think he had potential missing persons in mind. I doubt he envisioned this, exactly. At any rate, we had his explicit permission. Our attorneys vetted the paperwork."

Laurel's expression turned cool as she shifted into Agent mode. She knew that if she were going to help her family get through this, she'd need to maintain a certain emotional detachment.

"So, what you're saying is that our dad is Sarah's father?" she asked.

"Yes. We tested Linda's DNA as well, to be sure we knew the lay of the land. She's Sarah's biological mother."

"Did you test Owen's?" Laurel asked, although even as the words came out of her mouth, she knew that wasn't relevant.

"Yes."

Pieces of the puzzle began to fall into place. Sarah looked like the Danes. She had darker skin, thanks to her African American mother, but the resemblance was undeniable. They'd always joked about it growing up. Now, Laurel knew why.

Fourteen

"I THINK that's enough for today," Mikey said, standing. "Sis, let's get out of here."

Laurel paused, moving as if in slow motion. Her brain was struggling to keep up. When she turned to her brother, her face was a mask of seriousness.

"We can't just leave," she said. "There's a baby being held by kidnappers. We can't turn our backs on him. Especially now that we know he's—"

"He's what?" Mikey asked angrily. "I'm not so sure I'm convinced."

"DNA testing doesn't lie, Mikey," Brad added. "Results of Cornelius being Sarah's father came back at 99.99% confidence. That's a slam dunk."

They were all quiet for a moment as that sunk in.

Laurel looked at Brad. "How much are they asking for?"

"10 million."

"And it has to come from Mom?" Laurel asked. "Can't we just pay and say it's from her? I'm not sure she even has that kind of money."

"She has it," Mikey said reluctantly. He had been helping Maureen with her affairs since Cornelius' death. He was privy to her financial situation.

Brad shook his head quickly and shoved a hand through his hair. "Unfortunately, it has to come from her. And that's not all. Part of the demand is that Maureen be videoed admitting her Police Chief husband had an affair and a love child. They want Cornelius named and shamed. I'm not sure what they're trying to accomplish. We haven't determined if this is about the integrity of the police department or if it's a more personal beef."

Mikey balled one hand into a fist and punched the air. "This is insane. Do you realize that? $10 million ... and public shaming. Mom didn't do anything wrong. Last I checked, Dad wasn't here. This is cruel and unusual. Mom doesn't deserve this. Neither do Sarah and Linda, for that matter. Well, maybe Linda deserves it. I'd like to ask her a few pointed questions. Presumably, she's been keeping quite a secret for thirty-some years. Did Sarah know?"

"Sarah had no idea," Brad said, sighing heavily. "I'm sorry. Truly, incredibly sorry. I hate this like you wouldn't believe. You both know how I feel about the Dane family. I consider you my own and I'll protect you like my own. When it comes to this case, though, I've exhausted all of my options. Jasper's life is at stake. We have every reason to believe that the kidnappers will make good on their threat if Maureen doesn't cooperate. And we haven't had any luck identifying or locating them. Our hands are tied. Sarah is desperate for Maureen's cooperation, as you can imagine. She wants her baby boy back. Remember, she's a victim in this, too. She might be the one hurt the most, especially if we don't get Jasper home safe."

Laurel wiped away a tear. Her mom had been through so much already. This would crush her. Not only would the world know that Cornelius had been unfaithful, but he wasn't even alive for her to talk to him about it. Her questions would probably go unanswered.

"Does Mom know?" Mikey asked.

Brad shook his head. "Not yet. I'll be informing her shortly. I wanted to talk to the two of you first. You calling me from Jack and Jill's was good timing. The kidnappers have given us until Tuesday morning."

"I guess we should call a family meeting," Laurel said. "We should all be there when Mom hears the news. No point hiding it from anyone. This affects us all."

Brad nodded his agreement.

"Let the shit show begin," Mikey mumbled. He wasn't taking this well.

Brad pursed his lips and fidgeted uncomfortably in his chair, letting Laurel know there was something else. He had a good poker face around others, but not her. She seemed to break through his defenses. She was his one weakness.

"What else?" she asked.

"Since this is now confirmed to be a kidnapping case and a ransom has been demanded, we'll be working in conjunction with the F.B.I. As you know, Laurel, kidnapping—"

"Is a federal offense," she said, finishing his sentence for him. "Right. Have you told Jimmy about The Cradler?"

"Yes. Two agents are en route from the Nashville satellite office now. I'm not sure if they'll be the permanent assignments for the case, but they'll get us started," Brad explained. "Jimmy knows what's happening."

"Okay."

Laurel touched her lower abdomen absentmindedly. The world her baby would enter was becoming drastically different than the one she'd known just a few days prior. The *family* she'd known was becoming drastically different. Brad was close enough to his parents and one brother, but they lived in North Carolina. It was Laurel's big, boisterous family she thought of when she imagined their little one growing up around relatives.

Brad noticed Laurel's emotions getting the best of her, so he stood and walked around the desk. He crouched down on one knee beside her chair and wrapped his strong arms tightly around her. She didn't pull back, but instead, leaned into his embrace. Mikey turned and walked toward the window to give them a little privacy.

"Hey," Mikey said, reversing directions and heading for the door. "I need some coffee. Anyone else?"

"We're good," Brad said as Laurel sobbed quietly against his chest. "Pull the shades, would you?"

Mikey did as he was asked, then excused himself and slid out the door.

When they were alone, Laurel's sobs came harder. She clung to Brad, his familiar scent and the sound of his heartbeat a much-needed comfort. There were a million things on her mind, but she had a hard time finding words.

"Brad, I can't believe ..." she began, practically gasping for air.

"Shh," he said as he stroked her hair with one big, strong hand. "I know, babe. I know."

"How could Dad ...?"

Brad kissed her gently on the forehead. "I still believe that your dad was a good man. Maybe he made a mistake here. Maybe he had reasons to keep this a secret."

"Do you think he knew?" Laurel asked. "I mean, of course he knew that he had an affair. But did he know that Sarah was his? When I think about all the time she spent at our house when we were kids, I have to believe he didn't know."

"Maybe he suspected, but didn't want to rock the boat by raising the subject."

"What about raising his child?" Laurel asked, a tinge of anger in her voice. "Sarah grew up without a dad. From what she told me, he was never in the picture. She thought he didn't want her. How am I supposed to square that man up with the involved, caring father I knew? Would my dad really let a girl he suspected was his daughter spend the night and hang out at our home, then return to her mother's thinking she didn't have a father in this world?"

Brad shook his head, rocking Laurel in his arms at the same time. "What I do know is that I'm right here for you. Okay? I'm not going anywhere. I'll be by your side every step of the way. We'll figure things out."

Laurel nodded, feeling grateful for Brad's support. She needed him now more than ever.

"Okay," she said. "Thank you." He moved to pull back, but she clung to him even tighter. "Brad, now I understand why you kept this from me over the past few days. I'm sorry that I said I couldn't trust you. I get it now."

"Did you say that you couldn't trust me?" he asked jokingly. "I don't remember anything about that."

She smiled through her tears, appreciating his good nature.

"Well, there might have been an immature comment about Jamie," Laurel said. "Or two. I lost track."

"Let's not talk about Jamie," Brad said.

Laurel thought he was probably joking, but something in his voice made her wonder. She decided to ignore it, for now. She wasn't in any frame of mind to go digging for more drama.

She looked up at him and nodded. When their eyes met, the old spark they'd shared was there, stronger than ever. They stayed like that for what felt like forever. Until Brad slowly leaned in and pressed his lips against hers. His lips were warm. They sent shivers down Laurel's spine. Just like everything else about him, his kiss felt like home.

When they parted, Brad made it clear that he wanted more. "I'd like to come home to that every night," he said. "No doubt about it. I'd like you at my house. In my bed."

If she hadn't just heard something in his voice when she'd mentioned Jamie, she might have done exactly what he asked. As it was, Laurel needed to take things slow.

"I need some time," she said. "But I think I'll get there. Will you wait?"

Brad smiled, taking her response as a victory. "For you, my love, mother of my child, I'd wait a thousand years, walk a thousand miles ... whatever it takes. My world begins and ends with you."

Laurel smiled, then surprised herself by leaning in to kiss him again. This time, the kiss was more passionate. It lingered, and Laurel could feel it all the way down to her toes. It was as if she was coming back to life.

A mix of emotions swirled inside of her—anger at her father and at the kidnappers for putting them all through this, concern for Baby Jasper and Sarah, worry for her mom and the rest of her family who would be rocked by the revelation that Cornelius had another child, and now, renewed love and passion for Brad, the father of her unborn child. Brad was a good man. Now that Laurel understood why he was hiding things from her over the past few days, she could let down her guard and believe in his character.

She pulled back just as Mikey knocked on the door, two cups of coffee in hand.

"Come on in," Brad said, his arms still tightly around Laurel.

Mikey seemed more relaxed, like he'd used the time to collect himself. Laurel was relieved to see that.

"I'm okay, Mikey," she said as she wiped the tears from her face.

Brad wiped her tears as well, and she let him. There was a new level of intimacy between them. Mikey might as well know.

"Who's that extra cup for?" Brad asked.

"Eh, I downed one myself and brought these for the two of you," Mikey said. "You don't exactly have top of the line java available in this joint, but I thought you might need a pick me up."

Brad stood, and they took the coffee gratefully.

"Thanks, man," Brad said as he took a sip. "I've been meaning to implement an upgrade in the coffee department, but haven't quite gotten around to it yet. It's on my list."

Mikey nodded. "Yep."

There was a bit of an awkward silence as they drank. Everyone seemed to be adjusting to the new dynamic.

"So," Mikey began, "I called Jess and told her that I want her and the kids to head home without me today. They don't need to be here when all this hits the fan."

"Did you tell her what's going on?" Laurel asked.

"No specifics, just that a big family secret was about to be revealed. Luckily, we've been married long enough that she trusts me without asking too many questions."

Brad and Laurel glanced at each other when he said that. They both hoped they'd get to that point with each other someday.

"That's good," Laurel said. "I guess we need to get the van back to them so they can head out. I'll go ahead and get a rental car. Forensics will be processing mine for at least a few days."

Brad raised a hand. "Absolutely not. I'll drive my cruiser, and you can take my personal truck. What's mine is yours. I won't take no for an answer. You can swing by my house later and I'll make the switch."

"Thank you," Laurel said, without hesitation. "That will be great."

Mikey raised his brows. Laurel had told him that Brad offered his truck before. Her willingness to take him up on his offer now said a lot about how she was feeling toward her ex.

Brad smiled like the cat who ate the canary. Another victory. "Good," he said.

"Then I guess there's nothing left to do but call a family meeting," Mikey said. "Does five o'clock give us enough time? Ryan will have to leave campus in Murfreesboro. It's about an hour's drive."

Ryan was a professional pilot major in the Aerospace department at Middle Tennessee State University. He was probably relaxing, since it was a Sunday.

"He'll need to make arrangements for missing class tomorrow," Laurel said. "I doubt he'll want to go back to normal life right away, once he hears what's going on."

"Okay, then," Mikey said. "Laurel, how about you call Mom and Maggie? I'll call Ryan and Hazel. Make sure they know that it's imperative they attend. It's time for everyone to drop what they're doing."

"All hands on deck as we navigate through this storm," Laurel agreed. "Done."

THE RIDE back to Maureen's house from the police station was typically short. This weekend, though, probably due to the holiday, traffic was heavier than normal. Mikey groaned as he got stuck at every single traffic light on Main Street. This wasn't their day, in more ways than one.

Laurel and Mikey had called their family members. Luckily, everyone had understood the urgency and agreed to get together at five o'clock.

Brad had stayed at the station to get some more work done on the case before the family meeting, but he had sent Lilly home with Laurel. The dog was resting her chin on Laurel's knee as they rode along. Laurel stroked her head gently, certain the motion was soothing to them both.

"You're a sweet girl, aren't you?" she cooed.

Mikey smiled at his sister, despite his frustrated mood. "Aren't y'all a happy little family?" he asked.

Laurel opened her mouth to protest, but then stopped herself. Maybe he was right. And if so, perhaps she should embrace it. "I don't know," she said. "Maybe."

They chatted for a few minutes about all of the new people moving to town and how growing pains were inevitable. It was small talk, really, even though a more serious conversation was in order regarding the family orchard. That would have to wait. There were more pressing matters at hand. For all they knew, Maureen would go off the deep end and move to Florida to be near her sister. She'd have every right upon hearing that her husband had had an affair.

"How do you think this meeting will go?" Mikey asked.

Laurel hesitated before answering. "I'd like to say that Mom will handle the news with grace, but I honestly don't know. This will be a big blow."

"Yeah. I was thinking that maybe Sarah and her mom should be there."

"That wouldn't be fair to Mom, though," Laurel said. "Maybe we could bring them in later, but not when Mom first hears the news."

"Mom and Linda are friends, right?" Mikey asked.

"They're friendly," she replied. "I'm not sure I'd say they're friends."

"Well, they've known each other for a long time," he said. "I mean, you know Linda pretty well yourself, don't you? You've spent plenty of time at their house over the years. Especially growing up. I always thought you went to Sarah's for a sleepover when you wanted to get away from the rest of us." The corners of his eyes crinkled as he laughed. "I get it."

"That's true," Laurel said. "It was always nice and quiet at Sarah's house. Peaceful. What are you getting at?"

He twisted his mouth into a thoughtful position. "I'm not sure. Just thinking out loud, I guess. Maybe Mom will take it better since she knows Linda."

"Or maybe she'll feel like it's more of a betrayal coming from someone she knows."

"Yeah, that, too."

As they approached a railroad crossing in the middle of town, lights flashed and safety arms began to come down while the familiar dinging sounded its warning. Lilly stirred, concerned about the commotion. Laurel cracked her window so the pup could get a whiff of the approaching train. It was moving at a crawl, so there was plenty of time.

"Good thing we have a few hours before the family meeting," Mikey mused. "It seems like this town is conspiring to slow us down today."

"Are Jess and the kids waiting to see you before they leave?" Laurel asked.

"Yeah, I promised everybody hugs," he replied.

Laurel smiled. "That's sweet, Mikey. You're such a good dad."

"And husband. But I suppose I shouldn't toot my own horn."

"And husband," Laurel agreed with a laugh.

She was glad Mikey was staying in town for a few days. She needed her brother. She made a mental note to thank Jess for being so understanding and allowing her husband to take care of his family of origin during this crisis. Many wives would have insisted he prioritize her and their young children.

Laurel stared out the window as the train ambled along, lost in her own thoughts. She missed her dad. She wished he were here now to explain himself. As silly as it sounded, she also wished he were here to offer her advice. That gave her an idea.

"Hey," she said to her brother, "do you remember the mental screen trick that Dad taught us when we were kids?"

"The one where you imagine something you don't want on the screen and then slide it off and to the right to make way for the more desirable scene to enter from the left?"

"Bingo," Laurel said. "I actually used that technique during my F.B.I. training at The Farm. Did I ever tell you that?"

Mikey shook his head. "No, but that's interesting. I guess it works, huh? I've used it for weightlifting gains."

"Huh."

"What brought that to mind?" Mikey asked.

Laurel shifted her weight in her seat. "I was wishing Dad was here. I know it sounds odd, given the situation we find ourselves in, but I wondered what he would tell us to do. Like, what advice would he give us?"

"You think he'd have us use the mental screen to envision a good outcome?"

"Not that there's a perfect outcome here. People will be hurt, no matter what," she replied. "But we certainly want Baby Jasper to come home safe. Maybe we should visualize that."

Mikey nodded as the train finally passed and the safety arms went up. Lilly settled back down on Laurel's lap. She seemed satisfied with the distraction, which made Laurel wonder if the dog's previous owner used to take her for rides. If only Lilly could talk.

"If you think it will help," Mikey said. "I'm all for it. Want to do it together? We could have a group meditation session like we used to with Dad. That would be kind of nice, actually."

"Okay, but I'm not sure the others will want to join in when they first hear and are still processing the shock of the news. How about just you and me? Maybe later tonight after I get Brad's truck?"

"Or first thing in the morning," Mikey said. "You and Brad might be otherwise occupied tonight."

"Stop it," she replied, giving his arm a playful swat. "There's still a baby missing."

"I know, but your life can't come to a complete halt, Sis. You know that. You and Brad have to make up for lost time. From what I saw at the station a little while ago, you're both more than ready."

"We'll see," Laurel said with a smile. "Seriously, though, Mikey, I really miss Dad. I've been going through the motions as much as possible, but nothing is the same. I'm just sort of … numb."

"Me, too, Sis," he said. "I realize we're lucky to have made it to our thirties with both parents. Not everyone is as fortunate. It still sucks. I thought that old guy would always be there. I thought he'd live long enough to see my kiddos grow up. Maybe even meet his great grandchildren."

That stung, and Laurel visibly recoiled. "At least, he got to meet yours at all."

She cradled her abdomen protectively. The thought that her dad would never meet her baby hurt her deeply. The thought that he wouldn't walk her down the isle at her wedding was painful, too.

"Sis," Mikey began slowly, "I'm so sorry. I should have thought that through before I let it leave my mouth. Please, forgive me."

Laurel took in a jagged breath, fresh tears threatening to

emerge. Maybe it was pregnancy hormones—or the fact that she was still grieving her dad—but it seemed like she could cry at the drop of a hat lately. That wasn't like her.

She didn't reply to Mikey, but she gave him a half smile. That was enough. She wasn't mad at him. She certainly didn't want people to feel like they had to walk on eggshells around her. She'd deal with her feelings on her own, in her own time.

Mikey gave his sister's hand a squeeze. "I miss him, too. Terribly. Nothing is the same."

She nodded.

When they arrived at Maureen's and turned into the long, winding driveway at the bottom of her hill, they were immediately concerned by a pair of dark, unmarked cars parked near the house.

"What the hell?" Mikey asked. "Do those look like government vehicles to you?" He sped up, making his way to the top of the driveway as quickly as possible.

Laurel closed her eyes and shook her head, already fishing her phone out of her handbag. "Yes, they most definitely do. Dammit, Jimmy," she fumed as she dialed her boss' number.

"What makes you think he had anything to do with it?"

"Because I know him," she replied. "I should have predicted this. Once Brad told Jimmy that the F.B.I. was involved, Jimmy wouldn't be able to stop himself from running interference. It's how he's wired."

"I thought Brad said the F.B.I. people were coming from Nashville," Mikey said as he stopped the minivan and threw it into park.

"Maybe they did come from Nashville, but I'll bet Jimmy is responsible for jumping the gun instead of waiting until our family meeting at five o'clock," Laurel said.

The phone rang, but Jimmy didn't pick up. It went to voicemail.

"So, what you're telling me is that these agents will have told Mom before any of us have a chance?" Mikey asked.

"Probably."

"Which means that Jess and the kids are hearing all the sordid details as well."

"Yep."

"Dammit, Jimmy!" Mikey shouted as they got out and hurried in the front door.

"AGENT DANE, nice of you to join us," a familiar voice said as Laurel stepped into the foyer of her mom's beautiful home and took her coat off. She kept Lilly on the leash so that she could keep her close. She'd never been to Maureen's house before, and Laurel didn't have time to give the pup a proper tour.

The voice belonged to Jimmy Paulson himself, all the way from Washington, D.C. Laurel hadn't expected him to actually be here. His bald head glistened under the overhead lights, much like it always had in the office.

"Agent Paulson, what a surprise," Laurel said. "Didn't you have golf?"

Mikey closed the door behind them, then he and Laurel scanned as much as they could see of the rooms in the main living area. Jimmy was seated at the dining table in the formal dining room, nearest the front of the house. It said something about Maureen's frame of mind that she seated her uninvited guests there. The big farm table in the kitchen and at the back of the house was for family and friends.

Jimmy had two young agents on either side of him. Both looked green compared to Jimmy, his bald head and coarse beard framing his pensive eyes. Those eyes had seen a lot during his two and a half decades with the Bureau.

"Golf was yesterday. Keep up, Dane," Jimmy said with a laugh.

He stood and shook Laurel's hand, then Mikey's. Laurel made a hasty introduction.

Maureen sat across from the agents. She looked all alone on her side of the table, as if she was woefully outnumbered. It pained Laurel to see. Her mom seemed so delicate. So vulnerable. Judging by the look on Maureen's face, she had already received some bad news. Laurel couldn't tell for sure whether it was the bombshell revelation about Cornelius' infidelity, or something else. Jess and the kids were nowhere in sight.

"Where did my wife and kids get to?" Mikey asked as he walked over and kissed Maureen on the cheek.

Maureen gestured toward the guest bedrooms down the hall. "They're packing up to go back to Knoxville," she said, her voice strained. "Are you sure you want to send them home without you? Jessica looked madder than a wet hen when you called to tell her you weren't traveling, too."

"Absolutely," Mikey replied. "I'm going to hang around here for a few more days, if that's okay with you." He placed a hand on his mom's shoulder. "Jess understands."

"Okay," she said simply.

"I think I'll go say goodbye to them, though," Mikey said. "Will the rest of you wait on me for a few minutes? I'll be quick."

Jimmy hesitated, but Laurel nodded. "Special Agent in

Charge Paulson would be happy to wait. He's a very patient man."

The underlings smirked and Mikey excused himself, then left the room.

"Does Chief Tate know you're here early?" Laurel asked Jimmy as she walked around the table and took a seat next to her mom. "We had a family meeting scheduled for five."

Jimmy chuckled. "I know you've been on leave for a while now, Dane, but that's not how this works. I'm not required to keep the local police chief apprised of my whereabouts."

"So, the answer is no?" Laurel asked.

She was pushing the boundaries, and she knew it. She wouldn't normally talk to her boss this way. She was mad, though. How dare he approach her mom like this? Had he no sympathy? Besides, Laurel felt like she didn't have all that much to lose. If Jimmy was an ass to her family, that would make her decision to leave the Bureau easy. Brad would be protective, too. He wouldn't like Jimmy showing up early and verbally manhandling Maureen, which is exactly what Laurel got the sense that he'd been doing.

Jimmy scoffed. "If you want Chief Tate to know, then tell him yourself."

"I think I will," Laurel replied as she shot off a text to Brad.

> Jimmy and two baby agents here early.
> WTF? Mom looks distressed. Mikey and I
> just arrived. Can you come to the house?
> Please.

> On my way.

He replied within seconds.

Maureen closed her eyes and squeezed the bridge of her nose between her thumb and index finger. It was a pose Laurel had seen many times before when her mom had a migraine. Maureen's headaches were often stress induced. The way things were going, the poor woman would soon be in a dark room with a pillow over her head.

Laurel wanted to get her mom some pain medicine, but didn't want to leave her alone and outnumbered. She decided to wait until Mikey returned or Brad arrived before leaving the room.

"Brad will be here soon," Laurel said to her mom. When the baby agents looked confused, she added, "Chief Tate."

They nodded, then scribbled something on their notepads like dutiful students.

"Aren't you going to introduce me to your colleagues?" Laurel asked Jimmy. "Or should I say *our* colleagues?"

At that, the young agents didn't react. At least, Jimmy must have filled them in on Laurel's professional status. She was grateful for that much.

"Sure," Jimmy replied, playing along.

He gestured first to the female agent. She appeared to be of Middle Eastern descent with deep brown eyes and smooth brown hair cut neatly at her shoulders. It was obvious that she was intelligent. She tracked quickly and seemed to have a lot going on in her head. "This is Agent Samira Aziz," Jimmy said. Samira stood and straightened her blouse, then shook Laurel's hand.

Jimmy then turned his attention to the tall, muscular African American agent who looked like he could be a professional athlete. "This is Agent Malik Washington," he said. "Both are out of the Nashville satellite office."

"How do you do, ma'am?" Malik asked as he shook Laurel's hand.

It was silly, especially under the circumstances, but Laurel found Malik very attractive. If he weren't ten years younger than her, she might be interested in getting to know him more personally. Of course, there was Brad.

Stop it, Laurel told herself. It was probably pregnancy hormones. They seemed to be taking over her body—and mind—with a vengeance. She hardly recognized her own thoughts and feelings sometimes.

She cleared her throat. "I'm pleased to meet you both," she said. "I'd thank you for coming, but I'm not completely sure what you're doing here yet. I think I'll withhold my thanks for now. Until I learn more."

Samira smiled uncomfortably as she glanced at Maureen. Malik looked at the table in front of him.

Jimmy leaned back and cackled. "I see you haven't lost your sense of humor, Dane," he said. "Chief Tate *did* brief you on the situation, didn't he?"

"He did." Laurel wanted to ask how much her mom had been told, but she needed to tread carefully. This wasn't the way she, Mikey, and Brad had expected the day to go.

"Then you know we're taking over the kidnapping investigation. Kidnapping is—"

"A federal crime," Laurel said, finishing Jimmy's sentence. "Yeah, I'm aware."

Jimmy nodded.

"What does that have to do with me?" Maureen asked,

pounding one hand on the wooden table. "Why are you in my house?"

Mikey returned just in time to hear their mom's questions. He glanced at Laurel, and they both sighed with relief. Maureen didn't know yet.

Jimmy, always perceptive, realized what was happening and seemed to soften a bit. "Give me some credit, Dane," he said.

Laurel smiled ever so slightly, then took a breath and collected her thoughts. "Okay," she said. "Chief Tate will be here shortly. In the meantime, how about we offer you nice folks a drink? I'd like to wait for the Chief before we proceed."

Maureen seemed to like that idea, too. She relaxed a little and leaned back in her chair. She trusted Brad, and believed he had her family's best interests at heart.

Mikey moved toward the kitchen and took orders, then he prepared a tray with glasses of iced tea. Lemons, limes, and a few sprigs of mint sat in a ramekin on the side.

Maureen didn't keep unsweetened tea in the house. As was Southern tradition, all iced tea was prepared to be syrupy sweet. Laurel noticed that Jimmy almost choked when he took his first drink, but he managed to adapt quickly. Samira and Malik didn't seem fazed by the sweetness. Apparently, they had lived in the South long enough to become acclimated. Laurel wondered where they were from.

Lilly seemed to sense Maureen's anxiety. Even though they'd never met before, the pup leaned against the old woman's leg to offer her comfort.

"Is this Brad's dog that you told me about?" Maureen asked her daughter.

Laurel smiled as she reached down and gave Lilly a scratch behind the ears. "Indeed, it is. Isn't she a good girl? I'm already in love with her."

Mikey looked on proudly, glad to see his mom and sister talking about a happy subject, for the moment. The storm in their lives was coming. He wished to hold it off as long as possible.

Meanwhile, Jimmy was growing impatient. "I trust you folks know that our business here is urgent."

Laurel shot her boss a look of warning, but he didn't heed it.

"Do you think I had something to do with kidnapping that baby?" Maureen asked defensively. She was on edge.

Jimmy raised a brow and tilted his head to one side. "*Did* you have something to do with kidnapping that baby, Mrs. Dane?"

"Of course, not," Maureen said.

"Don't be ridiculous," Laurel said, at the same time. "My mother is a saint. She wouldn't harm a fly, let alone an innocent baby."

"Yeah, man," Mikey said, trying to keep his cool. "Our mom doesn't even get speeding tickets. She volunteers at the soup kitchen. She donates to local charities. She's squeaky clean. I promise."

Samira and Malik scribbled some more in their notepads, but neither of them made any comment.

"Why am I under scrutiny?" Maureen asked.

Jimmy shrugged. "I never said you were."

Laurel was just about to get firm in defense of her mother when she saw Brad's truck pull up out front. "He's here," she said as she stood and went to greet him at the front door. Lilly trotted along dutifully behind.

Everyone watched through the windows as Brad rang the doorbell. When Laurel opened the door to let him in, he scooped her into a warm hug and kissed her on the lips.

"Hey, babe," he said.

When he looked up, he realized that he hadn't taken time to read the room.

Laurel cleared her throat. She turned several shades of red, but decided that she wouldn't apologize. Why should she? Instead, she introduced Samira and Malik, then helped Brad get situated in the chair on the other side of Maureen. Now, with Brad, Laurel and Mikey beside their mother, the four of them outnumbered the agents on the other side of the table. That felt better.

"Okay," Laurel said to Jimmy. "We're ready to get down to business."

Seventeen

AS A KID, Laurel had been the peacekeeper in her family. A typical oldest child, she had taken on responsibilities for things that her younger siblings never felt obligated to get involved in.

It had won her the respect and admiration of her parents, but it had come at a cost. Even now, as an adult in her thirties with a baby of her own on the way, Laurel felt like she needed to take care of her mom and shoulder the burden that her dad's betrayal would cause. She knew it was messed up, but she had no real idea how to extricate herself from the dysfunctional behavior.

Maybe she was feeling especially emotional because it was now Christmastime, and the family would be facing the holiday without their beloved patriarch for the first time. Laurel ached for her dad. Hearing his favorite Christmas songs, decorating the family home, and taking part in time-honored traditions without him this year would be brutal. She imagined that her mom felt that ache, and then some.

At least, Brad understood. And he supported her, all the way.

"What are we doing here, at three o'clock, Agent Paulson?" Brad asked pointedly.

An uncomfortable silence filled the room as Brad made a show of glancing at his watch and then directing an icy stare at Jimmy. Laurel almost smiled, but she held it inside. She was grateful to Brad for taking a strong stand. She was sure that her mom felt the same way.

Maureen broke the silence. "When I looked outside and saw you agents at my door, I told my daughter-in-law, Jessica, to butter my backside and call me a biscuit."

Jimmy looked puzzled, so Laurel offered an interpretation. "She was surprised," she explained.

"Right," Jimmy said, meeting Brad's steely gaze. Jimmy wasn't rattled, exactly, although Brad's aggressive tone seemed to give him a moment's pause. "Well, we now have credible information that could lead to the safe return of Jasper Hobbs. We intend to secure the child's safety as soon as possible. The Federal Bureau of Investigation doesn't let family politics get in the way of our investigations. Agent Dane should know that better than anyone."

"Family politics?" Maureen asked. "I wouldn't kidnap no baby. Ask anyone who knows me."

Laurel and Brad both reached for Maureen's hands at the same time. They made eye contact and smiled when their hands touched over hers. Even under difficult circumstances, they couldn't help but smile at each other.

"We know that," Laurel said, refocusing her attention. "But Mom, there are a few things these agents need to ask you."

Mikey inhaled sharply. "That's right, Mom," he added. "And we're here to support you, okay? You're not alone in this."

Maureen looked concerned by her children's comments, but also comforted, at the same time. "Come out with it, then," she said.

Jimmy leaned forward, eager to keep things moving. He'd done this and worse hundreds of times. He wasn't shy when it came to breaking bad news. In this case, no one had been killed ... yet.

"Mrs. Dane, there's been a ransom demand that we believe is valid," Jimmy explained as Samira and Malik looked straight at Maureen with practiced expressions. "The baby is being held by a kidnapping syndicate led by a man known as The Cradler."

Laurel and Mikey held their breath, waiting to see how Jimmy was going to break the news, and waiting to see how their mom would react.

"Okay," Maureen said. "So, the baby will be safe, if you pay the ransom?"

Jimmy nodded slightly. "We believe so. Except that you have to be the one to pay the ransom."

Maureen's eyes went as wide as saucers. "Are you fixin' to tell me to pay ransom money? To *criminals*? A *Cradler*?" Her tone indicated just how preposterous she thought that idea was. "Why me?"

"The kidnappers have asked that you be the one to pay the ransom. If not, they've threatened to harm the baby," Jimmy explained.

"Kill the baby," Malik added, then cleared his throat. "They've threatened to kill the innocent baby."

Jimmy seemed slightly irritated by Malik's intrusion into the conversation, but he allowed it. "That's right," he said, shooting a look of warning the young agent's way.

"Why me?" Maureen asked again slowly, leaning forward.

Laurel squeezed her mom's hand. She wished there was something she could do to cushion this blow.

"Mrs. Dane, what I'm about to tell you might be hard to hear. It will probably come as a shock. Are you ready for that?" Jimmy asked.

Maureen looked from Laurel to Mikey to Brad, searching their eyes for answers. It was excruciatingly uncomfortable for all of them.

"Sorry, Maureen," Brad said.

Maureen leapt out of her seat, then paced at the back of the room. "Is this what you called a family meeting for?" she asked. "To tell me that the baby's life depends on me paying ransom money? Did everyone here know except me?"

Laurel stood to comfort her mom. She reached out to embrace her, but Maureen pulled back.

"Mrs. Dane," Jimmy continued, "please sit down so that we may continue."

Maureen bit her lip. "Don't try to make it sound like this isn't so bad," she said. "You can't make a silk purse out of a sow's ear."

Jimmy cocked his head to the side, but seemed to understand that phrase without Laurel having to interpret. He was getting used to Maureen's Southern way of speaking.

"Sit down, Mom," Mikey implored. "Please."

Finally, Maureen did. Laurel sat, too, and they all resumed their uncomfortable task.

Brad put a hand on Maureen's shoulder.

Jimmy took a deep breath. "Mrs. Dane, were you aware that your husband, Cornelius Dane, had a relationship with Linda Peterson and that he fathered her daughter, Sarah Peterson?"

There. It was out. Nothing could stop it now.

Maureen sat silent for what felt like an eternity. She blinked, so they knew she was in there. But was she processing the information? Or was she too shell shocked to speak?

"Mom?" Laurel asked.

Maureen stood quickly, the chair toppling to the floor behind her. In dramatic fashion, she stomped out of the room and headed for the back of the house. The others weren't sure what to do.

"Should we follow her?" Brad asked.

"Give her a minute," Mikey said.

"Agreed," Laurel added.

Jimmy leaned back in his chair and ran a hand over his bald head. "Agent Dane, time is of the essence here. Do I need to remind you—?"

"You do not," Laurel said. She was protective of her mom, and she didn't want Jimmy pushing her around.

"We have until Tuesday morning to pay the ransom to this Cradler character, right?" Mikey asked.

Jimmy nodded. "Yes, but—"

"Then we can give her a minute."

"Fine. Five minutes," Jimmy said as he, too, stood. "You mind if I smoke on the front porch?"

Laurel waved him on, then he stepped outside and lit one up. It was a nasty habit that Laurel wished her boss would abandon, especially now that she was pregnant. She did not want to be breathing that poisonous stuff and exposing her baby. Today was not the day to debate it, though. She just hoped Jimmy knew better than to leave cigarette butts on her mom's porch.

As they all waited, a full-size silver SUV approached. It moved slowly but deliberately up the driveway.

"Who is that?" Mikey asked.

"No idea," Laurel said. "No one that I know."

Brad stood and looked out the window, then turned to the agents. "Are you folks expecting anyone?"

"No," Samira replied.

The vehicle was a Grand Wagoneer. They all watched as it came to a stop at the top of the driveway, behind the growing number of other cars, trucks, and SUVs parked in front of the house. It was a good thing Maureen had plenty of room.

Jimmy took it upon himself to welcome the man who exited the vehicle. "Good afternoon," he said as he put out his cigarette.

The man grunted in reply. He was older—somewhere around Maureen and Cornelius' age—but fit and strong. He had piercing blue eyes and a white beard that still bore a lot of red around the mustache area. He was wearing a tan hat with a wide brim to accent a blue flannel shirt covered by a mustard-color flannel coat.

"That's a lot of flannel," Laurel remarked as she watched through the window.

The man moved with purpose. He grabbed a leather satchel bag from his backseat, then lowered his gaze and walked to the front porch. He hit the lock button on the keyfob, causing the shiny new vehicle to beep and flash its lights.

"You think he's selling something?" Mikey asked.

"Does he look like he's selling something?" Brad replied.

"Definitely not," Mikey said. "I dunno, man. I'm just spitballing here."

The front door opened, and they heard Jimmy ask the man what his business was.

"My name is Mack Roberts," he said. "I'm here for Maureen. She's expecting me."

Laurel's eyes practically popped out of her head upon hearing this. A quick glance at Mikey and Brad confirmed that they shared her surprise

Laurel turned to call out for her mom, but Maureen was already there, greeting her guest at the front door.

"You made it," Maureen said warmly as she stood on her toes and wrapped her arms around Mack's thick neck.

Mack leaned down and kissed her on the lips as he dropped his bag on the floor at his side and wrapped his strong arms around her. Something about the way his big hands looked on Maureen's trim waist made the scene feel almost too intimate for the others to be watching. "I booked a flight as soon as you called, Reenie. I'm here."

"Reenie?" Laurel asked.

Laurel wasn't sure she'd ever seen her mom that affectionate with her dad. Not for many years, anyway. What was happening? Who was this man? Mack. The name fit him. He was built solid, like a Mack truck.

Maureen touched a finger to her lips, savoring the spot where Mack had planted a kiss. Then she took one of his hands and led him into the dining room. Jimmy followed behind.

"Everyone, this is a special man in my life, Mack Roberts," Maureen explained. "We've been dear friends for years."

"More like I've been madly in love with her for years," Mack said, giving Maureen a swat on the rear end. She giggled like a schoolgirl. "Ever since Mr. Gregory's World History class in high school," he continued.

Laurel and Mikey both felt like they should say something, but they were too stunned. They'd never heard of this Mack Roberts. Had their mother been having an affair? The entire world seemed to be turning upside down.

Brad filled the silence for them. "Welcome to Appleman's Gap," he said. "Although, it sounds like you're from here." He extended his hand for a friendly shake, which Mack accepted.

"That's right. Born and raised, until I graduated high school and left for Colorado," Mack explained. "I've been there ever since. My feelings were too hurt when Reenie took up with Cornelius instead of me. I kept in touch with her over the years, hoping there'd be an opportunity for us to get together and set things right. Finally, my patience has paid off."

Maureen giggled again, which was strange for her. She wrapped her arms around Mack's broad shoulders. It seemed like the two of them needed to get a room. Wasn't she just crying over her dead husband?

"I'm sorry," Laurel said, "forgive my bluntness, Mack. As you might imagine, this is a bit of a shock."

He nodded approvingly. "Go ahead. Say what's on your mind. You're Laurel, right? I've seen pictures of all of you kids. Ask me anything you want."

"Let's sit," Maureen said.

Eighteen

"I FEEL like someone should pop some popcorn," Jimmy said as he returned to his seat.

No one laughed, even though they wanted to.

The others sat down in their seats as Maureen hung Mack's coat and hat in the entryway, then dragged a chair beside hers for him to sit in. She placed it on Brad's side, which saved Laurel the awkwardness of getting up close and personal with her mom's new man right off the bat. You could have cut the tension in the room with a knife. The air was practically buzzing with anticipation and unanswered questions. Maureen took Mack's hand as they settled in beside each other.

"Mom, when you asked Mack here, did you know?" Laurel asked.

"Know what?" Maureen asked innocently. Her demeanor had done a one-eighty since Mack arrived. She was smiling now, seemingly unbothered by the news about Sarah.

"What these agents came here to tell you."

Mack looked puzzled, so Maureen filled him in. "That my —Cornelius—fathered a child during an affair."

"That lowdown bastard," Mack grumbled. He looked like he wanted to punch something. Or someone.

"And ... that his illegitimate daughter's child has been kidnapped," Maureen continued as Mack looked pensive. "The bad guys want me to pay the ransom. I guess they want to embarrass the family. Lord only knows for sure—and he ain't tellin'."

Laurel persevered. "Mom, did you know?"

"Know what?" she asked.

"You're being evasive," Laurel replied. "Why?"

"Evasive?" Maureen asked. "Am I getting Agent Dane right now? Because I'd rather talk to my daughter."

"How about being honest with me then?"

Maureen pursed her lips, twisting her mouth this way and that while staring down at Mack's hand as it clutched her own. The others didn't dare say anything and interrupt. They all wanted Maureen to come clean and tell them the truth.

Finally, she spoke.

"That Sarah was his daughter?" Maureen asked, then paused dramatically. The room hung on her every word. "Yeah, I knew. Don't piss on my leg and tell me it's rainin'."

Mack chuckled. He, too, apparently, knew that Sarah was Cornelius' daughter. No wonder he didn't seem to have a high opinion of the man.

"You what?" Mikey asked, standing.

Just as he did, they saw Jess and the kids moving around in the back of the house and heading toward the side exit. Mikey paused only momentarily as he blew them a kiss and told Jess he'd call her later. She gave him a knowing look, but didn't ask any questions. He returned his gaze to his mom as he waited for her to answer.

"Don't get all upset," Maureen said to her son. "I'm not the one who did the dirty deed. Your outrage should not be directed at me. Tell your father, if you have a problem."

"It's a little hard to do that, since he's *dead*," Laurel said. It was childish, she knew, but she was angry and didn't know how to act.

Brad gave her a sympathetic look, but he didn't seem all that surprised. Maybe he'd seen enough as a cop that this kind of thing didn't faze him anymore.

"Did you know about the ransom when you called him?" Laurel asked.

"My name is Mack," Mack added. "You can call me by my first name."

Laurel ignored him, but stayed focused on her mom. "Well?"

Maureen shook her head. "No, *that* I didn't know until y'all told me a bit ago. I asked Mack here because I was sick of sitting around and being sad about a man who had disrespected me for years. It wasn't good for me, and I knew I needed to move on. I always knew that someday, it would be Mack and me. It was time."

It occurred to Laurel that they must have witnessed her mom and Mack's first kiss when he came in the door. At least, the first since high school. She didn't want to think that her mom might have had an affair, too. It was all too messy. Too scandalous. If you'd asked her a week ago whether either of her parents had been unfaithful, her answer would have been unequivocally no.

"What was all that talk about how you didn't have

enough time with Dad?" Laurel asked. "And how you just wanted to be with him, his hand in yours? How quickly you got over that," she mused as she glanced at Maureen and Mack's hands that were still joined.

Brad sighed, sorry to see Laurel in pain.

"Yeah?" Mikey added.

"That was true," Maureen replied. "It is true. But it's also true that your dad was a cheater. I'm happy to be free of that. I'm ready to move forward."

Laurel shook her head and raised a hand to cover her mouth. She thought she might cry. She was so far from the Agent Dane persona now that it made her head spin. The series of personal blows had been too much.

Jimmy drew in a breath, then leaned forward and placed both elbows on the table. "I realize this is a lot for you all to take in," he said, "but we're here because a baby's life is in danger. I'd ask that we turn our collective attention back to the task at hand."

Laurel scoffed. "That's true," she said, frustrated. "We can't let that baby get hurt because of our bullshit family drama."

"Yeah," Mikey agreed.

They hadn't told Maureen the eye-watering amount of the requested ransom yet. They also hadn't told her that the kidnappers wanted her to be filmed saying that her husband was a cheater. She might not go for any of that. It was a big ask.

Mack stiffened, his chest rising with pride. "How much do they want? I'll write a check."

Maureen beamed at his show of chivalry. "Mack is a

retired dentist who still owns a booming practice with multiple locations in Denver," she explained.

"I'd write a check, too, if it were that simple," Brad said.

Laurel appreciated his sentiment, but she knew Brad wasn't made of money. He came from a humble, working class family, and although he'd made some smart investments in stock over the years, he wasn't what most people would consider wealthy.

"Why isn't it that simple?" Mack asked. "I'm good for it. Tell me an amount. What? Do you need the money in cash?"

Jimmy leaned even further forward. "To the tune of ten million dollars."

The color drained from Maureen's face. "They must think we're shittin' in high cotton over here."

Mikey shrugged. He knew his mom had the money.

"That isn't all," Jimmy continued. "Mrs. Dane—"

She interrupted. "Please, call me Maureen."

Jimmy nodded his understanding. "Okay, Maureen. The Cradler has demanded you be filmed stating that Cornelius Dane had an affair which resulted in the birth of a child, and further, that Jasper Hobbs is Cornelius' grandchild."

Laurel was still trying to process the fact that her mom knew about Sarah. Had she always known? There were so many unanswered questions.

Maureen scoffed. "You've got to be kidding me. I did nothing wrong. Why do these people want to see me suffer?"

Mack looked pained. He rubbed one thumb over Maureen's palm. "I'm here, Reenie. We'll get through this."

Maureen smiled at him, but it did little to ease her distress.

"They insist that the money come from you," Brad

added. "There are specific instructions they say we have to follow, if we want the baby returned safely."

"I'm sorry, Mom," Laurel said. "I know this is a tough pill to swallow."

Before they could discuss the matter further, they heard a key in the front door. In walked Ryan, Maureen and Cornelius' youngest son. He had driven back from college in Murfreesboro.

"Hey, there," Ryan said, unsure what to make of the scene. He kept his coat on, frozen much like a deer in headlights.

"Come in, son," Maureen said, then she went to give her boy a kiss on the cheek.

Ryan was barely twenty, and although he was mature for his age, this situation would be overwhelming for him. He needed to be involved, though. It wouldn't have been right to exclude him. It was time for him to grow up fast.

"Hey, Mom," he said, giving her a hug. "Who are all these people?"

Maureen began to make introductions, starting with Jimmy, Samira, and Malik. She hadn't quite gotten to Mack when the door opened again.

This time, Maggie and Hazel walked in. The entire Dane clan was here now.

"Hey, Mom," Maggie said as she hugged her mother's neck. Younger sister Hazel did the same.

Hazel was the shyest of the bunch, which was strange since she ran the apple barn and country store for the family. She was good at her job, but she relished her downtime when it was over each day. Her long brown hair cascaded down around her shoulders and framed her angular face. Hazel had a toughness about her that the other siblings didn't. Laurel often thought she would have been good in law enforcement, too.

"Brad!" Hazel exclaimed. The two of them had always been buddies. She was clearly glad to see him again. "Good to see you, big guy."

Brad smiled and nodded, then winked at Laurel. He was happy to be back with the Dane family. He wished it were under better circumstances.

Mikey took it upon himself to make the introductions this time as Maggie and Hazel hung their coats and found seats. The room was getting crowded. Any more guests and they'd have no choice but to move to the bigger table at the back of the house.

When it came time for Mikey to introduce Mack, he hesitated.

"I'm in love with your mother," Mack said, filling the pause. "I fell in love with her in high school and haven't been able to shake her hold on me, all these years. I live in Denver, but I'm here to make a life with Reenie, if she'll have me."

The younger Dane siblings looked shocked, but not entirely. Laurel couldn't help but wonder if they knew something she and Mikey didn't. They had stayed in Appleman's Gap, after all. Perhaps there were signs that Laurel and Mikey would have seen, if they hadn't moved away.

"You never married anyone?" Maggie asked. Leave it to her to be direct.

Mack's face was serious. He looked as if he was at the most important job interview of his life.

"Once, in my twenties," he replied. "We had one son. I

love him dearly, but the marriage didn't last long. What can I say? She was a good woman. She wasn't my Reenie."

He clasped Maureen's hand again, and she beamed.

Wishing to get back on track, Jimmy steered the conversation. "Okay, now that we're all here, let's move forward. I'm sorry if I sound insensitive, folks, but we have a kidnapped baby to save. We need Maureen's cooperation, and as soon as possible."

Maureen looked at her kids. "They want ten million dollars and me to go on camera and say that your dad had an affair."

Maggie, Hazel, and Ryan didn't flinch.

"Wait," Laurel said. "You all knew? About Sarah being Dad's daughter?"

They nodded slowly, hesitant to do the wrong thing or upset anyone.

Mikey was visibly upset. He shoved a hand through his blonde hair. "Wow," he said. "Move away to make a life for yourself and get iced out of the family. Why keep Laurel and me in the dark?"

Laurel crossed her arms over her chest. "Let it be, Mikey. That's the least of our worries right now."

PART THREE

Family Secrets

FOR THE NEXT SEVERAL HOURS, the group talked through various scenarios as Maureen sought a way to avoid paying the ransom. She admitted she had the money, but that it would clean her out and make operating the apple orchard for the upcoming year difficult. Mack offered to pitch in up to five million, and said he could get the rest, if given a few extra days to liquidate assets. Jimmy reminded them all that the clock was ticking, and that the money had to come from Maureen.

Maureen deeply resented the fact that she was being taken to task for Cornelius' poor choices. She wished he was still alive so she could give him a piece of her mind. She continued to hold Mack's hand tightly as she hemmed and hawed about her predicament.

As the day wore on and dinner time approached, they all grew restless and hungry.

"I'm so hungry my belly thinks my throat's been cut," Maureen said. "How about we break for a while and I order some food?"

They agreed, and Mikey got on the phone to order meat and threes from Puckett's Restaurant. Puckett's was a favorite in the Nashville area. They had just opened a location in Appleman's Gap, and Maureen had been wanting to try them.

Mikey ordered plenty of food, figuring they could eat the leftovers another day, if there were any to be had. Chicken and dumplings, chopped steak, and pulled pork were all on the menu, plus mashed potatoes, coleslaw, macaroni and cheese, potato salad, Southern green beans, and smoked baked beans to choose from on the side.

Once that was done, Jimmy asked Laurel if he could speak to her privately outside.

"What's up?" she asked as they settled into a pair of chairs on the front porch. The sun had set and it was much colder. Laurel had to go back inside to retrieve her winter coat.

When she returned, her boss didn't mince words. "I need you to be straight with me. Is your mom going to cooperate? Because if not, I've got to make other arrangements. I don't have to tell you how important this is."

Laurel nodded. "I get it. Jasper's life is on the line. Now that I know he's my nephew and Sarah's my sister, I want even more to bring him home safely."

"What do you think she's going to do?" he asked. "I get the sense that your mom might not play ball here."

Laurel took a long, deep breath. "I get that sense, too. I think she's mad at my dad, and she doesn't want to pay that much money or be embarrassed on video. I think she feels like this isn't her problem."

Jimmy exhaled sharply. "That's what I was afraid of."

"I assume you're doing everything possible to find The

Cradler and thwart this whole thing, right?" Laurel asked. "Has the Bureau made any progress in identifying him?"

"None yet," he replied. "But yeah, we have people working around the clock. These kidnappers are clearly professionals. Our usual methods aren't panning out. These crooks know how to play us."

"It sounds like we need more time," Laurel said. "I learned at The Farm that the simplest solutions are often best. Can we talk these guys into giving us more time? Tell them because they're asking for so much money, it will take a while to access. That's the God's honest truth. Ten million is a lot."

"I'm not sure the Petersons would want their baby in the hands of The Cradler any longer than absolutely necessary."

"Of course, not. But we also can't force my mom to cooperate. Can we?" Laurel asked.

"No, we can't."

Jimmy sat quietly for several minutes, thinking.

"You know," Laurel began, "I realize I'm too close to this and that closeness is dulling my instincts, but something about the whole thing makes me believe there's a bigger motive than just money. The apology request is personal. And making Mom appear on video when the affair was Dad's doing? That's vindictive, in a twisted way."

"I've got the same read on the situation," Jimmy agreed. "Our profilers are working on it. Until we can identify The Cradler, it doesn't do us any good, though. Unless you know something you aren't telling me?"

Laurel crossed her arms over her chest defensively. "I know nothing. Quite the opposite. I get the sense that other people know things they aren't telling me. You included."

"You mean the thing about Sarah being your dad's love

child?" he asked. "We kept that from you for less than a day, and we did it to protect you."

"What if I don't want to be protected?"

"What if you need to be protected?"

"I don't," Laurel replied, "but hearing you say that only makes me think there's more you're hiding. Is Brad in on whatever it is, too?"

Right on cue, Lilly stuck her nose out the door. Brad followed closely behind. He'd taken her off the leash, which Laurel wasn't completely comfortable with. She chalked it up to being pregnant and vulnerable. She held her tongue, trusting Brad to know how to keep his dog safe. She'd have to trust him with their baby before too long. She might as well start giving him the benefit of the doubt in that department.

"Hey, man," Jimmy said, dropping the tough guy act. It was just the three of them now. Friends.

"Hey," Brad said. "What are you two talking about out here? Anything I can help with?"

Jimmy shook his head. "Just that we don't think Maureen's going to cooperate. She's sympathetic, but she doesn't feel ownership. The stakes aren't high enough for her, personally, as compared to the cost."

"Which is terrible, since a baby's life is in danger," Laurel added.

Brad positioned himself beside her chair and put an arm around her shoulders. His hand came to rest low on her chest. He didn't try to hide it from Jimmy, who raised his brows in acknowledgment. Lilly settled at their feet.

"I agree on all counts," Brad said. "What are we going to do?"

Jimmy shook his head again. "Laurel says to ask for more time."

"Not a bad idea," Brad replied. "Did your team process the car yet?"

"Happening as we speak."

"Maybe they'll find something we can go on," Brad said. "How about the tech people? Any leads?"

"Nothing yet," Jimmy replied. "Like I told Laurel, they're working around the clock. We have all of our resources on this."

Laurel hadn't been involved in a kidnapping case of this magnitude before, but she knew the Bureau would take it seriously due to the size of the ransom demand and the fact that other babies had been nabbed. At least, that's what Officer Martin had said on the phone the night she called from the trunk of her car. He'd said that mothers had been taken, too.

"Question," Laurel began, "when I talked to dispatch the other night from the trunk, the officer told me a few details. It seemed like he was telling me out of respect for my dad. I don't know. Maybe it was simply that I'm an agent. Anyway, he said that other kidnappings had been happening at places where a baby is left inside a vehicle unattended for a few minutes. He also mentioned missing mothers and a couple of bodies. Are there other cases that might be connected to this one?"

Brad and Jimmy made eye contact, an unspoken understanding between them. Brad didn't seem to want to answer, but Jimmy wasn't going to do it.

"There are," Brad said. "I don't want you to worry, babe. Jimmy has all of our case files."

Laurel fumed at the way she was being treated. When she had learned about Sarah's paternity, she foolishly hoped that was all Brad was keeping from her. Obviously not.

Damn him.

At the same time, though, she loved Brad and needed his affection now more than ever. Couldn't he be forthcoming with her? Was that too much to ask?

A heavy silence hung in the air as the men waited to see how far Laurel would push the issue. Deciding that she genuinely believed both Brad and Jimmy had her best interests at heart, she let the subject drop. For now.

"Fine. I won't worry, then," she said.

Brad visibly relaxed. Jimmy was better at hiding his reactions, but he seemed relieved, too.

"What's next?" Laurel asked.

Jimmy had, apparently, been thinking about that very question the entire time. He had an answer ready. "I'm going to communicate with The Cradler and ask him for more time. It's a risk, but it's one we have to take. Assuming we can convince him, we'll need to work on Maureen. Maybe her new man can help turn the tables."

Laurel scoffed. "Don't get me started on Mom's new man," she said.

"He seems nice enough," Brad said. "I recognize a man in love. I think he's completely dedicated to making Maureen happy."

"Will you talk to him?" Jimmy asked. "Give me time to work on my end of things."

"I can do that," Brad said. "It can't hurt and it might help. It's worth a shot."

"Good man," Jimmy said to Brad. "I'm going to ask for

another week. We'll see how that goes. If we're lucky, we'll crack the case and apprehend these assholes before the week is up."

"Assuming they don't decide to up the ante," Laurel said.

The thought sent a cold shiver down her spine. She'd never forgive herself if something happened to Baby Jasper. She still felt responsible for allowing him to be taken in her car and on her watch. She should have been able to keep him safe.

"Right," Jimmy said, standing.

Jimmy shot off a few texts to various underlings, but he stayed long enough to be there when the Puckett's delivery arrived. He let Maureen fix him a plate, which he took with him when he left. Samira and Malik did the same.

Everyone else stayed put, piling on couches in the living room after dinner. Maureen was thrilled by the prospect of having more time to deal with the ransom demand. She hoped the F.B.I. would catch The Cradler and eliminate the need for her to fork over ten million dollars.

The family had a lot of catching up to do, and a lot of getting acquainted with Mack Roberts.

Twenty

"CAN I TRUST YOU?" Mikey asked Brad.

The younger siblings had gone to bed for the night when Mikey, Brad and Laurel found themselves alone in front of a crackling fire with a bottle of wine. Lilly dozed peacefully on the rug in front of the fireplace without a care in the world. Laurel wasn't drinking, of course, but Mikey and Brad were enjoying the Merlot.

Maggie and Hazel had each headed home to their own places and Ryan had gone upstairs to his room right there at Maureen's house. Ryan lived in a dorm in Murfreesboro, but still had a room at home to stay in during college breaks. Maureen and Mack had retreated to the master bedroom, which felt strange to Laurel and Mikey. What would their dad say, if he were alive to know about this? How quickly he was being replaced.

"Yeah, you can trust me," Brad replied. "You ought to know that. Why do you ask?"

Mikey looked around to be sure no one else was listening.

He lowered his head and his voice. "Because I'm going to hack into F.B.I. servers."

Brad's face contorted into a ball of confusion. "You're what?" he exclaimed.

"You heard me."

Laurel leaned forward, her elbows resting on her knees. "Mikey, that's insane, even for you. Do you have any idea how many layers of security the internal servers are behind? Or how many years in solitary confinement a stunt like that would get you?"

"Relax," he said. "I'm not going to tamper with anything. I want to know what they know."

"Mikey, I have access," Laurel said. "I am the F.B.I. Have you forgotten? I can probably find out what they know with a little digging. I might get a slap on the wrist if I go too deep, but you will most certainly get imprisoned if you do."

"That's only if I get caught."

"Mikey, I don't—" Brad began, but Mikey cut him off.

"Don't give me the boy scout routine," Mikey said. "This is my family we're talking about. Something bigger is going on. I don't know what it is, but I know I have to find out. It's time for me to step up and make things happen."

"Mikey," Laurel said, "I'm the oldest sibling and the F.B.I. agent. Please, let me do this. I'm thinking about leaving the Bureau, anyway. I'm willing to take risks. I completely agree with you that there's more going on. And that it's time to take it into our own hands. But let it be me."

Brad shook his head and sat straight up in his seat. He dropped his hand from where it had been resting on the small of Laurel's back. "This is my family, too, and I won't have either of you in trouble. I mean it."

Laurel appreciated what Brad was trying to say, but Mikey was right. Someone outside of law enforcement had to make things happen. Maybe it did need to be Mikey. Maybe his plan was the only good one, under the circumstances.

"How would you do it?" she asked her brother.

"I wouldn't tell either of you the specifics," Mikey replied. "I trust you, but I don't want you knowing anything that could come back to bite you. I have some friends out there. With their help, I'd poke around and see what I could find."

"Like on the dark web?" Laurel asked.

"Well, that sounds cooler than it actually is, but something like that," Mikey replied.

"You realize you'd have the N.S.A. to deal with as well?" she asked. "F.B.I. and N.S.A. servers are monitored by the United States Cyber Command."

"I'm familiar," Mikey said with a sly smile. He was familiar with such matters, and his sister knew it.

Brad looked more distressed than Laurel had ever seen him. He stood, then shoved a hand through his short, dark hair.

"Easy, Captain America," Mikey said as Brad began to chew his lip. "This won't come back on you."

"It's not that," Brad said. "Did it ever occur to you that if you go digging for trouble, you might find it?"

"What's that supposed to mean?" Laurel asked, wrinkling her nose. "If I didn't know any better, Brad Tate, I'd think you were still hiding something from me."

She stood, too, and approached him from behind. She wrapped her delicate arms around his waist and leaned her head against his back. He softened at her touch. The embrace made them both remember that they'd be alone at

Brad's house soon. Laurel still needed to drop Brad off at his house so that she could borrow his truck. She intended to spend a little time inside. In fact, she'd been thinking about it all day.

Mikey got the drift, and decided they should table the hacking discussion until tomorrow. It was getting late, anyway.

"Look, I've got to get some rest," Mikey said. "How about we talk again in the morning?"

Brad's phone dinged. It was a text from Jimmy.

Good news. The Cradler agreed. We have another week. The Petersons are livid, but that's to be expected. By the way, this guy is a real piece of work. He wears a gold baby rattle on a chain.

"Wow," Brad said as he read the text. "That's shocking. The Cradler agreed to another week. Luck must be on our side."

"Let's hope it stays that way," Mikey replied.

Mikey excused himself and headed upstairs to bed, leaving Laurel and Brad to decide what the rest of the evening would hold.

"Give me a few minutes, then we'll go to your house, okay?" she asked.

Brad smiled from ear to ear, his body language happy and relaxed. "Babe, I'd wait on you forever. Take as long as you need."

Laurel smiled, too, then went to her bedroom to freshen up. Lilly followed along, hopping up on an easy chair while Laurel washed her face in the en suite bathroom. Lilly was taking a shine to Laurel, and the feeling was mutual. The two of them hoped to spend a lot more time together.

Brad hadn't invited her yet, but Laurel suspected she might want to stay overnight at his house. Just in case, she threw a few things in a duffel bag—a change of clothes, basic toiletries, a charger for her new phone, and a bottle of Brad's favorite perfume. She thought about bringing her laptop, but decided against it. She needed more time away from the stressful demands of life as an agent.

Tonight, she wanted to be just Laurel. Brad's love. She wanted to rekindle their connection.

"There," she said to Lilly. "I'm ready."

Lilly raised her head and woofed her approval, which made Laurel laugh.

Brad must have been waiting eagerly, because he stuck his head in the door. He eyed the bag Laurel had packed. "What are you two girls talking about?" he asked.

Laurel smiled coyly. "That's for us to know."

"And me to find out?" he asked as he scooped Laurel into his arms.

Brad let his lips rest just inches away from her neck. She could feel his warm breath on her skin, and it delighted her senses.

"Maybe," she replied playfully. Then she turned and picked up her bag. "Are we leaving, or what?"

"Don't let me slow you down."

Lilly seemed to smile, too. She acted like a kid who was happy that their parents loved each other. That's what all kids wanted, Laurel supposed.

The three of them made their way to Brad's truck, then they trekked across town like the perfect little family. Brad drove, Laurel rode in the passenger seat, and Lilly sat in the back with her front legs perched on the center armrest. Soon, their baby's carseat would occupy the middle space in the back. Lilly would have to move over or find a new spot.

Laurel felt guilty for being happy when Baby Jasper was still out there in the hands of bad people. She thought about what Mikey had said, that her life had to go on. She knew he was right, but allowing herself enjoyment was easier said than done.

Brad seemed to know what she was thinking. He reached over and took her hand, then brought it to his lips and kissed it. "Hey, don't beat yourself up. I see the wheels turning in that pretty head of yours. Take a night off, okay? For me? You can go back to worrying about Jasper first thing tomorrow morning."

Brad was right, too. The two of them had often talked about how hard it was to put their professional stressors aside and live their lives. It was always that way. Work in law enforcement meant a steady stream of upsetting situations and cases that took hold and wouldn't let go. This one was far more personal than most, but the tenets were the same. This career would make you crazy, if you let it.

"I'll try," Laurel said. "It isn't just Jasper. It's Mack and the ransom and Dad and—"

Brad put a finger to Laurel's lips, prompting her to pause. "Tomorrow," he said. "For tonight, forget all of that. You can't solve any of the problems right now. You're officially off duty. I said so."

He smiled that jovial smile of his. The one that kept Laurel in good spirits, no matter what. The one she wanted to see every day, for the rest of her life.

As they pulled into his driveway, Laurel felt herself tense. That was the opposite of what Brad wanted. "Hey," he began, "Jamie isn't here. She went to visit an aunt in Birmingham for a few days. Relax, okay?"

That did the trick. She closed her eyes, letting the tension melt away. Lilly stood up and licked Laurel's cheek, as if to reassure her that everything would be all right. The pup's kisses made Laurel giggle.

"You silly girl," she said softly. "You're good at cheering people up, you know that?"

Taking her change in demeanor as a good sign, Brad got out of the truck, then walked around and opened Laurel's door. He extended his hand, which she took. He kept his palm on the small of her back as they walked inside. Lilly followed closely behind.

Once in the warmth of the indoors, Lilly became focused on her food and water bowls. She ate and drank like she was starving, oblivious to anything else happening around her. Brad took the opportunity to concentrate on Laurel. He put his keys and wallet down on the kitchen counter, took his bomber jacket off, then helped Laurel out of her coat. The air between them was positively electric as he wrapped his arms around her waist from behind and she eased against him.

"You didn't stay long enough for a proper tour the last time you were here," he said, kissing her neck slowly between words. "I suppose I should show you around."

Laurel's entire body tingled. She wished she could stay right here, wrapped tightly in Brad's protective arms, forever. "You're right," she replied with a laugh. "I didn't even see the bedroom."

Taking the hint, Brad reached down and lifted her at the

knees. Then he carried her down the hall and to the bedroom, like a bride being carried over the threshold. He was a big, strong man. Laurel's weight was nothing in his arms. When he got there, he placed her down gently and propped himself over her, his body positioned between her knees.

"You kept things the same," Laurel said. "Like at your condo in D.C. It's all here."

The wooden, king-size bed with horizontal planks running the length of the headboard and footboard, the pick stitch quilt in blues and whites, the room-darkening window panels in steel gray hung on clunky wooden rods. Everything felt comforting to Laurel. It was a soothing sight for sore eyes.

Brad nodded. "I thought you'd like it that way, if you ever came to visit. Besides, it reminded me of home. *Our* home."

Brad's condo in Alexandria, Virginia is where they'd spent most of their time together. They'd even decorated it together, choosing furnishings that suited their shared tastes. When they'd broken up, Laurel had rented an apartment. It didn't feel like home. That's surely one of the reasons she took an extended leave and retreated to her mom's house in Appleman's Gap. Seeing everything here, in Brad's new home, which just so happened to be located in her hometown, was a dream come true. One she didn't even know she wanted.

"I love it," she said as she stretched toward Brad and kissed him passionately. "I've needed this. I've needed you."

"Not as much as I've needed you, my love," he said as he returned her affection. "You showed up here like an angel, sent from heaven above. You're the answer to my prayers. I've been on my knees."

"Oh, yeah?" she asked, moving her soft hands over his body between kisses. "Maybe I should get on my knees?"

Brad pulled back for a moment, a huge grin on his face. "I thought I was the one whose mind ventured to the gutter more often than not. Look at you."

She shrugged. "I blame the pregnancy hormones."

Smiling so big their cheeks practically hurt, they held and caressed each other as they made sweet, tender love. When they were finished, they talked for a long, slow while.

"It doesn't get any better than this," Laurel mused as she let herself fall peacefully asleep.

THE NEXT MORNING, sun shone low through the plantation shutters in Brad's bedroom. He was already gone from the bed when Laurel woke. She was disappointed, but she understood. It was Monday morning and there was much for the Chief of Police to tend to. He'd be hers again at the end of the day. He was worth the wait.

She felt around for her phone, but found Lilly instead. The pup was nestled against Laurel's legs, her snout tucked against one knee.

"Good morning, girl," Laurel said. "We're becoming buddies, aren't we?"

Lilly sighed, as if to say she agreed. She wasn't ready to be disturbed, though. She grumbled like an old man when jostled. Laurel decided the dog must not be a fan of mornings.

Finding her phone on the nightstand beside her, Laurel checked to see what she'd missed.

There was a text from Brad professing his undying love and apologizing for having to leave so early. She replied that it was perfectly okay, and that last night had been one of the best, ever. All felt right in the world, now that they were back together. Were they back together? Laurel made a mental note to discuss that with Brad as soon as possible. She was ready to make it official.

There was another text from an unknown number that Laurel soon realized was Kanesha.

> Hey, Laurel, I'm off work today and think I might have found something else that would interest you. Can we meet?

> By the way, this is Kanesha. In case you didn't know.

> Hey! Awesome. Can it wait until this afternoon? I have some things to take care of this morning.

Remembering Mikey and their mention of a meditation session, Laurel was hesitant to make morning plans with Kanesha. She also felt less stressed about the kidnapping case now that they knew more about what they were facing. Her task was to convince Maureen to pay the ransom. She had an extra week to do it.

> I don't mean to be pushy but I don't think this can wait. Meet me at Gap Grounds Coffee Co.? Nine o'clock?

Laurel agreed, but she wanted to grumble like Lilly. It wasn't anything against Kanesha. She liked the woman and genuinely hoped they would become friends. Laurel was simply growing weary of living with such high adrenaline. Maybe pregnancy hormones were to blame for that, too, but she longed for a more peaceful life. Once they got Baby Jasper back and closed this case, that's exactly what she intended to find, if at all possible.

She texted Mikey, who said he'd meet her at the coffee shop. Now that Laurel had Brad's truck at her disposal, getting around would be much easier. She assumed Kanesha wouldn't mind Mikey tagging along. Laurel felt like she could use Mikey's eyes and ears to help her keep up with the rapidly changing situation. Also, she had a hunch that Mikey had begun poking around in government servers. She didn't want to waste any time in finding out what he'd been up to. He was an early riser. For all Laurel knew, her brother could have infiltrated the F.B.I. already.

After a shower in Brad's bathroom—which Laurel was beginning to think of as hers, too—she got dressed and spent some time in the backyard tossing a ball for Lilly while she waited for it to be time to meet Kanesha and Mikey. The day was cold, but not quite as cold as it had been over the holiday weekend. Temperatures were back up to the mid-fifties. That was normal for Appleman's Gap this time of year.

She looked around Brad's yard between tosses, appraising the home and his decorating skills. It was a nice place. Given the cost of living difference, he probably pocketed a nice chunk of change after selling his condo in D.C. He'd made a good investment in Appleman's Gap. The house was in good shape. The location was excellent, too. Laurel could see herself living here. Raising their baby here.

She'd just need to take care of one issue first: Jamie Beck. That woman had to go. Regardless of what Brad said about their relationship—or lack thereof—she was trouble. Laurel could see that a mile away. The line of Jamie's crop top was just a little too high, the dip of her neckline a little too low. The way she applied her eyeliner, the plumpness of her lips ... she oozed sex appeal, and not in a way that made a man think about marriage and family. Jamie was a temptress. Laurel wanted her to move out of Brad's guesthouse. Immediately.

"Don't let the door hit you on the way out," Laurel mumbled. "Right, Lilly?"

Lilly woofed, as she had taken to doing whenever Laurel asked her a question. Laurel didn't think the pup actually agreed. She probably liked Jamie just fine. Her move was happening, though, whether Lilly approved or not.

After a few more tosses of the ball, Laurel took Lilly back inside. She loaded her up with treats and promises for more snuggles and playtime that evening.

Even though she hadn't discussed it with Brad, she knew it was okay to stay at his place again tonight. He had kissed her as he'd given her a key and told her to make herself completely at home. Laurel thought she might even pack a few suitcases and move her things to Brad's house permanently. If she were going to stay in Appleman's Gap, she'd have to rent a truck and bring her things home from D.C., of course. For now, she could set up at Brad's instead of her mom's place. What with Mack at Maureen's, Laurel wasn't too keen on hanging around there, anyway. Maybe she should invite Mikey to stay at Brad's, too.

"See you tonight," Laurel told Lilly as she locked the door behind her and pulled it shut. "Be a good girl."

Lilly accepted her fate and settled onto the sofa where Brad had placed the dog's favorite fleece blanket. She had a great view of both the front and back doors from that spot. She could even see out the large picture window at the front of the house that overlooked the front yard and the street beyond.

"Good girl!" Laurel said again, through the closed door.

Then she climbed into Brad's truck and cranked it up. He'd scooted the seat forward for her, knowing that she'd need it closer to the pedals than he did. Brad was thoughtful like that. His simple gesture made Laurel smile. Those were the little things that made for long, healthy relationships.

"Good man, Brad," she said out loud as she stroked the seat lever affectionately.

It was then that Laurel considered talking to their baby for the first time. She hadn't felt him or her kick yet, but based on the baby books she'd read, that would happen soon. Could the baby hear her if she talked to it? She wasn't entirely sure, but the urge was there so she did it, anyway.

"Baby, you have a good daddy. You'll be hearing his voice a lot more over the weeks and months to come. He loves you so very much. I love you so very much, too. That daddy of yours, though, is one of the best. I picked a good one for you. You can rest easy, knowing that much for sure."

She smiled and touched her lower abdomen.

She hadn't been to an OB since leaving D.C. If she was going to hang around Appleman's Gap long, she should see someone here, just in case she had a problem or question and couldn't reach her doctor out of state. The doctor who came to mind was Sarah's who had delivered Baby Jasper. Dr. Elsa Stewart was superb.

Feeling inspired, Laurel picked up the phone and searched for her number, then gave the doctor's office a call. The receptionist who answered said they had an opening, if Laurel wanted to make an appointment. She surprised herself by saying that she did. With that confirmed, Laurel felt accomplished. She had done something for herself and her growing family. All of the people who had told her to take care of herself would be proud.

"There, baby," she said, giving her abdomen a pat. "We have an appointment. Daddy will be glad to hear it. Your Uncle Mikey will, too."

Uncle Mikey sounded good to Laurel's ears. He was the only one of the Dane siblings who'd had children, so there wasn't anyone to call him Uncle Mikey. Until now.

Satisfied, she backed the truck out of Brad's driveway and drove across town to Gap Grounds Coffee Co. It wasn't far—nothing was in Appleman's Gap—but traffic was busy and it took a good fifteen minutes to get there.

When she arrived, she could see Kanesha through the front window. Mikey was already there with her, and Laurel noticed her mom's gold Buick parked a few spots over. She had completely forgotten that Jess took their minivan back home to Knoxville. She should have offered to pick her brother up.

"Hey," Laurel said as she entered the coffee shop. A bell above the door rang ceremoniously. "Hope you aren't having too much fun without me."

It was crowded inside the coffee shop, but not so much as to necessitate them going somewhere else. The place had been selling coffee and donuts to residents of Appleman's Gap since Maureen and Cornelius were kids. Laurel liked supporting their business. The owner had recently retired, and his son had taken over. Rumor had it that he was considering expanding to a second location. He was also thinking of setting up Gap Grounds coffee carts in the local grocery stores.

Mikey laughed. "Never."

Kanesha greeted Laurel cheerfully, and had already gotten her a bottle of water from the barista. "I know you said water only at Jack and Jill's," Kanesha explained. "Do you want anything else?"

"Water is perfect," Laurel said. "I'm avoiding caffeine, for the baby's sake."

"So, you definitely *are* pregnant?" Kanesha asked. "I didn't want to pry, but it was pretty obvious."

Laurel chuckled. "Indeed, I am. Hardly anyone knows, though. You're one of the first."

"How special," Kanesha replied.

They chatted for a few minutes about various topics, until Mikey finally steered the conversation to more serious matters.

"Hey, Kanesha," he said, "Laurel said you had something to share with her. I hope you don't mind me listening in as well?"

"Not at all," she said. "You're going to want to hear this."

<h1 style="text-align:center">Twenty-Two</h1>

"THERE'S a guy I think you should keep an eye on," Kanesha said, leaning forward and talking quietly so the people seated nearby wouldn't eavesdrop.

"Okay," Laurel said. "Who?"

"I don't know his name. You'll have to figure that out yourself, but I saw him at the apple barn with your sister."

Laurel was surprised. She hadn't mentioned a sister to Kanesha.

"Which sister?" Mikey asked. "I have three."

Technically, he had four now with Sarah, but he wasn't ready to count her just yet.

"Hazel," Kanesha replied, clearly keeping up.

As Kanesha spoke, Laurel began to hear classical music again. This time, it was Schubert's Ave Maria. A cello took the lead. It reminded Laurel of a time during her Air Force Band days when a famous cellist had been featured as a soloist. More importantly, hearing the music meant that an important clue was about to be revealed. They were onto something.

Laurel shot her brother a look to let him know about the music, but she wasn't sure he received the message. She'd tell him later, when they eventually discussed what had taken place this morning. The music was her cue. It was remarkable, but it was a private, personal experience. She'd never met anyone else who experienced the same thing.

"How did you know about the apple barn?" Laurel asked Kanesha.

"I looked you up," Kanesha said. "It's all right there on the internet. I hope you don't feel stalked or anything. I enjoy crime type stuff. I've been watching it on TV for as long as I can remember. *CSI*, *Law & Order*, and *NCIS* are some of my favorites. I almost always solve the case before they do. Anyway, I had a hunch, so I went to your family's orchard. I tried to look inconspicuous. Bought some fried pies and apple cider. Delicious, by the way."

"Yeah?"

"Yeah," she continued. "I met Hazel and her cats. Crook and Chase, right?"

Mikey chuckled. "That's right. You aren't from around here, so you probably don't get the reference. The cats are named after a duo who used to be on a country music talk show in Nashville. Lorianne Crook and Charlie Chase. It was one of our dad's favorites, so we grew up knowing about it."

"I see," Kanesha replied. "I wondered if Chase was because the cat chased mice or something. Maybe Crook stole the other one's food. Who knew? Good to clear that up." She laughed, then tossed her long braids over one delicate shoulder. "So, I posed as the new girl in town, which I am. I chatted with Hazel for a while, then browsed and watched when she got busy."

"Did you see something interesting? You mentioned a guy." Laurel asked. Ave Maria continued to play in her mind, intensifying as Kanesha talked. This was going to be good. She knew it.

Kanesha raised her brows up and down. "I sure did. There was a twenty something guy hanging around. He was skinny ... and greasy. Blonde hair so light it was almost white. Long hair, too, down to his waist in a ratty ponytail. Looked like he might be on some kind of drugs. I don't mean to make assumptions based on his looks alone, but he acted twitchy, too. You know? Like a tweaker or something. Whatever the term is. I was never into drugs, so I don't know all the names they're called."

Laurel and Mikey nodded.

"I saw him with Hazel at one point. He kissed her and had his arms draped around her waist from the back. It was creepy."

"Did it look like they were together? Dating?" Mikey asked.

"I didn't think she had a boyfriend," Laurel said. "She hasn't mentioned one to me."

Kanesha wrinkled her nose. "Have you ever seen memes about men that hang on a woman's back like that? Something about that pose gives the impression that the guy is taking advantage of the girl. Like maybe he doesn't work or have any money. I'm just talking now, and I should probably stop making judgments. I'm just saying it was weird. Something was off."

The music crescendoed even further, filling Laurel's ears. It was so loud that she had a hard time believing no one else heard it.

"Did you see anything else?" Mikey asked.

"Yeah," Kanesha said, nodding. "When Hazel got busy with customers at the counter, our guy let himself into the back office. I didn't see any other employees except for a crew working in the orchard outside. No one else was in the office when he was in there."

"That shouldn't have happened," Laurel replied. "Our dad used that office. No one has been in it much since he died. I assume his documents and other business items are still there. Did you watch what the creepy guy did?"

"Yes, but I couldn't tell much. He was on the computer. The way the window was, I couldn't see his hands on the keyboard, but it looked like he put something in his pocket when he was done. Maybe a thumbdrive."

"What would he want with that?" Mikey asked. "I'm not sure how apple orchard business is interesting to anyone. What could he possibly be seeing?"

"Maybe Dad used the computer for more than apple orchard business," Laurel said.

Kanesha let them talk. She seemed eager to help, but also like she felt uncomfortable intruding in their family business.

"Dad was a good guy," Mikey mused. "You aren't saying he was doing something shady, are you? That would have been way out of character for him."

"I don't want to think so either, but we should probably consider all possibilities. Whatever is happening that's being kept from us could be more complicated than we think," Laurel said.

"You think there's something being kept from you?" Kanesha asked, her eyes alight.

Kanesha was finding this a thrill. She obviously enjoyed

investigating, and she was good at it. The thought occurred to Laurel that Kanesha would make a great assistant if she ever became a private investigator. Kanesha was a natural.

"Maybe," Laurel said, unsure how much she wanted to share.

"There's something else," Kanesha said. "Something I found."

"Go on," Mikey said.

Kanesha reached into the pocket of her jeans and pulled out a folded up piece of paper. She handed it to Laurel without unfolding it. "Here. Please don't shoot the messenger."

"How did you get this?" Mikey asked as Laurel carefully opened the paper.

"The guy must have printed it out. I saw him put it into his coat pocket, so I pretended to accidentally bump into him and I pulled it out."

"Wow," Mikey said. "That's impressive."

Laurel gasped so loudly when she read what was printed on the paper that it practically made her choke. She tiled the page to show Mikey.

There was a printout of a passport. It had Cornelius' photo and looked official, but the name and address were fake. At least, Laurel and Mikey *thought* the name and address were fake.

"Dennis McCready?" Laurel asked.

"With an address in Sullivan's Island, South Carolina," Mikey added. "That's the Charleston area, right? Didn't you stay there on vacation once?"

Laurel nodded. "Yeah, Brad and I spent an Easter weekend in a vacation rental there. Beautiful spot on a quiet beach. Dogs are allowed, and they like to play in the pools that form when the tide goes out. I remember because seeing all the pups made Brad and I talk seriously about how we wanted to get a dog one day."

Mikey smiled. "And now you have Lilly."

"Aww," Kanesha cooed.

"But why would Dad have a passport with some fake identity? And if he did, why would he keep a digital image of it on the computer in the apple barn?"

"And how would the greasy guy know where to find it?" Kanesha asked.

"Good questions," Laurel said, the music in her mind reaching a fever pitch. "I need to tell Brad. And Jimmy."

"Who's Jimmy?" Kanesha asked.

"My Special Agent in Charge at the F.B.I.," Laurel explained. "He's in town working the case. Kidnapping is a federal offense."

"I think he wanted to get involved because of Laurel," Mikey added. "He seems like a good guy, and he cares about you, Sis. He's kind of like a big brother. Isn't he?"

"If my big brother was sour as grapes," Laurel said with a laugh. "But, yeah."

"Okay, well, you do what you gotta do," Kanesha said. "I have some more time today. I think I'll keep digging."

That probably was a good idea.

"Keep your phone on," Laurel instructed. "They'll want to interview you. They will probably want your help identifying the guy you saw, too. Maybe they'll even have you work with a sketch artist. It depends on how much information we get from Hazel."

"I got a good, long look at him," Kanesha replied. "I knew to look carefully. I even took some notes."

"Good work," Laurel said.

Kanesha was about to stand, but before she could the bell above the door chimed with the arrival of new guests.

"Oh, shit," Laurel said when she saw Sarah, her mom Linda, and her boyfriend Owen enter the coffee shop.

She'd wanted to reach out to Sarah, but now that she knew they were biological sisters, it was awkward. Laurel wasn't ready. Yet, there was no way to sneak out the back and avoid a confrontation. They had already made eye contact.

Laurel grabbed her brother's hand and squeezed it tightly. He knew Sarah and her family well. He instantly understood how difficult this would be for Laurel. It wouldn't be easy for him, either. Sarah was the sister he never knew he had.

"What's happening?" Kanesha asked, confused by everyone's reactions.

There was no time to explain. "Hang around a minute and we'll tell you after, or go and we'll tell you later," Laurel said. "Up to you."

Kanesha opted to go, promising to get in touch later as she held her cup of coffee and scooted out the door. She said a polite hello to Sarah, Linda, and Owen as she walked past. A look of recognition washed over her face when she saw them up close. She must have pieced it together. Or maybe she had seen their faces on the news. Either way, Laurel would explain it to her later.

"Hey, Sarah," Laurel said across the crowded room. "How are you holding up?"

It wasn't the right thing to say. There wasn't one right

thing to say. Laurel knew that, but it felt uncomfortable coming out of her mouth.

Deciding that actions would speak louder than words, Laurel stood and went to her friend, then hugged her. Sarah seemed shocked by the encounter. She didn't hug Laurel back. Instead, her arms hung limp at her sides.

"Give her some space," Owen said, moving in between the two women.

Owen Hobbs was a muscular, handsome African American man with strong features and deep brown eyes. For several years, he and Sarah had dated on and off. Laurel had never been the biggest fan of Owen's due to his inability to get and keep a good job that would support Sarah and Baby Jasper, but she knew that was none of her business. Especially now. She wasn't even sure if she and Sarah would remain friends. How could Sarah forgive Laurel for letting her baby be kidnapped.

Linda Peterson, Sarah's mom, was the one who'd had the affair with Cornelius Dane and kept it a secret all these years. She's the one Laurel was mad at. What kind of person lets their child grow up not knowing who their father is? Unless Sarah had known. Laurel didn't think so.

Mikey joined them, appearing at Laurel's side just in time to rescue her. "Wonderful to see you all," he said as he handed Laurel her coat and handbag. "We were just on our way down to the police station to see what we can do to help."

"Is there a break in the case?" Linda asked eagerly.

"We'll leave that to the police," Mikey said.

"If your mom would pay the damn ransom, we'd have Jasper back by now," Linda said angrily.

Her tone didn't sit well with Laurel or Mikey. Linda was

awfully condescending for an adulterer. Had she forgotten her part in this mess?

"Great," Mikey replied as politely as he could manage. "Have a good day, folks."

"Take good care of yourselves," Laurel added as her brother guided her around a group of people and to the front door.

Every single one of them felt worse for having seen each other. Such was life in a small town. There was nowhere to run or hide.

Twenty-Three

BY THE SAME time the next day, Laurel and Mikey arrived at Leopold's, the local diner where Brad had gotten takeout the night of the kidnapping. The prime location on the main drag in town made it an easy meeting spot.

Tourists often thought the place was named for the infamous historical figure, but really, it was the namesake of the owner, old Leopold Nunnery. He was in his eighties, but still showed up to work for at least a few hours each morning to make sure things were trucking along as they should. The coffee was always hot, most of the breakfast menu was cooked in a cast iron skillet, and the fruit pies were legendary.

The siblings had agreed to eat together this morning, and they were hungry.

"Good morning, kids," Leopold said with a wave as they entered.

Cornelius had taken the Dane clan to Leopold's on Saturday mornings for years, right after cartoons on TV. They were usually ravenous by then, and Leopold always knew how to make sure they left satisfied with full bellies and a smile.

"Good morning, sir," Mikey replied. "How's life treating you?"

Leopold waved him off. He was polishing a coffee pot behind the counter. They both knew he'd stop by their table to chat later.

A morning meeting was becoming Laurel and Mikey's routine. Laurel had been at Brad's again last night, and the siblings needed to compare notes.

"Have you talked to Hazel since they took her in?" Laurel asked before she had even taken off her coat. "Brad said they questioned her for several hours yesterday afternoon."

It was dreary outside—cloudy with intermittent drizzle that made things feel depressing. Luckily, Christmas decorations were being hung around town, which helped brighten the dark days. It was officially the first day of December, and the town Christmas parade was scheduled to happen on Saturday.

"No. You?" Mikey asked.

Laurel shook her head. "I sent her a text, but no response. I'm not sure she knows my new number."

"Or maybe she's pissed at us," Mikey said.

"I wouldn't be surprised. Especially if she considers this guy her boyfriend. She probably feels like we threw him under the bus."

"Right. Because if she thought he was on the up and up, she would have brought him to Mom's house, don't you think?" Mikey asked. "Hazel has brought plenty of boyfriends around in the past. Why hide this one from us? She could have even invited him to Thanksgiving dinner. But yeah, I'll bet she's good and mad."

"Sounds like he would have needed a shower first," Laurel said with a laugh. "Kanesha described him as kind of nasty."

Mikey laughed, too. "Speaking of our friend Kanesha, have you heard anything else from her? I suspected she would have found more clues by now."

"Not yet, but I thought the same thing. Give her a few hours. I'm sure she'll have something else to add. She really does have a knack for investigating," Laurel explained. "If I ever do move back home and become a private investigator, I'd hire her in a minute."

"Are you actually thinking about moving back?"

Laurel shifted her weight, her hand coming to rest on her lower abdomen. It was a move she caught herself making a lot lately. It was strange to be so connected to her baby when it was still a tiny little thing that probably didn't even look human yet.

"Maybe," she replied. "I mean, I want Brad to be involved, and he's here."

"You want him to be involved with the baby, or you want to be with him?" her brother asked.

Laurel blushed. "I want to be with him."

"Then I guess that settles that. Mom will be thrilled," Mikey said.

Laurel took a deep breath. Mikey made it sound so simple. She was coming to the same conclusion, but she hadn't fully admitted it to herself. Washington, D.C. had been her home for a long time. It felt like she and Brad had belonged there. Adjusting to the idea of them belonging in Appleman's Gap would take some doing.

"It would be nice to be near family. You and Jess could move the kids back, too."

"Easy now," Mikey said. "We're settled in Knoxville. But it would be great to have you a few hours away instead of an entire day's drive. We could see each other a lot more often. My kiddos would like to know their little cousin."

A young waitress whose name tag read Ginger arrived with glasses of water, then took their order. She must have been new in town because they didn't recognize her. She was friendly enough, though, and her hair and freckles matched her name. Being health conscious, Laurel ordered a bowl of oatmeal with fruit and nuts. Mikey opted for an omelet filled with everything under the sun, including enough meat and cheese to clog a man's arteries, if he wasn't careful. Once Ginger scooted off to the kitchen, the siblings got busy reviewing progress on the case.

"Brad's having lunch with Mack Roberts today," Laurel said. "He's going to do what Jimmy asked and enlist Mack's help in convincing Mom to pay the ransom."

"I hope it works. I hate to see Mom turn over that kind of money, but what's the alternative? We can't let an innocent baby die. Our nephew, no less," Mikey said as he took a big swig of water.

"I don't think there is an alternative, unless authorities find The Cradler before the deadline. That means they'd have to find where Jasper is being held, too. If The Cradler is as smart as we think he is, he'd have the baby in a different location," Laurel said. "Although, that could be a good thing. I doubt that Jasper is the only baby who has been taken. I get the sense this isn't a one time event for this creep."

"Unfortunately, I think you're right," Mikey replied. "It's sickening. There are better ways to make money, even for criminals."

"Agreed."

"What did Brad think about the dude Hazel was with? Did they find the guy?" Mikey asked.

"Not as of this morning when Brad left for work. They have a strong lead, though. He seemed hopeful they could bring the guy in today."

An old man at the jukebox popped some coins and Nat King Cole began singing "Caroling, Caroling." It felt odd to carry on with the festive holiday season when such a horrible situation was unfolding for Jasper and his family. At the same time, though, it was Laurel's first holiday season as a mother-to-be, and she wanted to enjoy it. Next year, she'd have a bouncing baby in her arms to celebrate the season with.

"Does it feel to you like he's family?" Laurel asked, thoughtfully. Again, she touched her abdomen, a silent connection to her own little one.

Mikey pursed his lips, considering the question. "It's weird, but yeah. It kind of does. He's our blood. Regardless of how shitty I think it was that Dad cheated on Mom and had a baby, I can't bring myself to blame Sarah or Jasper for any of that. They're innocent. They're victims. They didn't ask for any of this."

"Yeah," Laurel replied, "we should probably reach out to them at some point. As a family, you know?"

"It'd be nice to welcome them to the Dane clan and let them know we have their backs," Mikey said. "I don't think we'll get Mom on board with that anytime real soon, but maybe the rest of us could be a united front. If Hazel will speak to us."

"Right."

They sat silently for a moment, the enormity of their situation weighing on them both. Laurel wanted to ask if her brother had done any hacking, but she knew that it might be better if he didn't tell her. He was still in town, which meant he thought he could help. Otherwise, he would have headed back home to Knoxville by now.

"So, what's our next step?" she asked. "Are we ... taking things into our own hands?"

Mikey laughed. "Is that code for something, Sis?"

"Come on, Mikey. Don't make me spell it out," she replied with a chuckle.

Mikey smiled that devilish grin of his, but didn't answer.

"Okay," Laurel said. "I'll go first. I did some digging on Dad's fake identity. The address in South Carolina belongs to a real estate investor. The property is usually advertised and rented for short-term vacation stays, but it's been off the rental market for six months now. I have a call in to the owner. He lives in the Bahamas, and his secretary tells me he functions on island time. I'm not sure how fast he'll call me back."

"Good for you," Mikey said. "Anyone on the ground in South Carolina who can pay a visit?"

"I thought about that. It's too far for me to travel without staying a few days," Laurel said. "I don't have the energy I used to. Plus, I want to be here for Mom and Sarah. For whatever they might need. I'd toyed with the thought of hiring a private investigator down there to check it out. What do you think about that idea?"

"As in, someone who can knock on the door and see if Dad answers?"

Laurel was surprised to hear those words come out of her

brother's mouth, even though the same had occurred to her. "Do you actually think that could happen?" she asked.

Mikey ran a hand through his hair just as Ginger arrived to deliver their food. She set the warm plates down on the table, then pulled two rolls of silverware out of her apron pocket.

"Need anything else?" the young woman asked.

"Do you have any milk?" Laurel tried.

"Yep. Cow's milk, oat milk, almond milk, and soy milk," Ginger replied.

"Wow!" Laurel exclaimed. "Leopold is stepping up his game. I'll have almond milk, please."

"Ketchup would be great for me," Mikey added.

Ginger left, then returned quickly with their items. Their food was still piping hot by the time she had them taken care of. She refilled their glasses of water, too. Pleased with herself, she returned to the kitchen.

"Are you really going to eat all that artery-clogging mess?" Laurel asked her brother.

"Not every day. I'll have to get back on my bike soon to make up for it, but today? You betcha," he replied.

She smiled, pouring the almond milk on her oatmeal and adding a sprinkle of brown sugar. "I admit that the six month time period gave me pause. But that's crazy to think Dad could be alive. Right?"

"What did Brad say?" Mikey asked.

It was a good question. Laurel still felt like Brad was keeping things from her. She believed his intentions were noble, which was the only reason she wasn't angry with him about it.

"I didn't tell him yet," she replied.

Mikey paused between bites of steaming omelet to raise his brows and express his shock. "I thought you two were good. Shouldn't you be working as a team?"

"We should," she agreed. "Let's just say we were otherwise occupied last night. I'll tell him when he gets home this evening."

"Now that's the spirit," Mikey said. "Otherwise occupied is good. So is you calling his house home. I'm happy for you. But seriously, Brad might be able to help."

"Yeah, you're right."

"What else do you have?" Mikey asked. "Jimmy and his team get the car processed yet? I see you're still driving Brad's truck."

Laurel shook her head. "Not yet. It takes time. They're doing all they can. Now, your turn. What have you found?"

Mikey shrugged, making exaggerated chewing noises. "I've been trying to steer clear of Mom and Mack's PDA. Ryan, too. Poor kid. I think he's going back to school tomorrow. He's been stuck with the brunt of the Mom-and-Mack situation. He feels like there's nothing he can do to help, anyway."

"You're avoiding my question," Laurel said.

Mikey chewed some more, practically inhaling the rest of his omelet in a few big bites. When he was finished, he wiped the corners of his mouth with his napkin and drank more water.

"Okay, okay," he said. "I'm working on something. For now, I'll leave it at that. When there's something solid to share, I promise I'll let you know."

Before Laurel could finish her oatmeal, a string of police vehicles came screaming down the main road in front of the diner. Their sirens were blaring and their lights were flashing. They were headed east out of town. They turned off on a state highway, then crossed the old bridge heading to a remote area known as Cedar Hollows. Though she couldn't be certain, it looked like Brad's cruiser was leading the charge.

"Should we follow them?" Mikey asked.

"No." Laurel squirmed uncomfortably in her seat, the spoon clanking against her bowl as it dropped to the table. "Ask anyone who has experienced a trauma what their worst nightmare is," she mused. "They'll tell you they're afraid of the same thing happening again."

Twenty-Four

LAUREL'S BREATH fogged in the cool air as she hurried across the parking lot towards Brad's truck, the early winter haze cloaking everything in shades of gray. Mikey had left a few minutes earlier as Laurel stayed behind to use Leopold's restroom. She had intentions of heading back to Brad's place for an afternoon nap with Lilly. The pregnancy was taking its toll on her energy reserves. She needed to make time for extra rest.

With no pressing leads to follow and much of the police force occupied with whatever was happening in Cedar Hollow, Laurel felt there was time for an hour or two of shut-eye. She returned to Brad's house, took Lilly outside for a potty break, then cuddled up with the pup under a fleece blanket on the sofa. She turned on a daytime talk show in the background, although she wasn't really watching.

Before she drifted off to sleep, Laurel sent a text to her mom. Laurel and Brad had promised Jimmy they'd try to convince Maureen to pay the ransom.

Can Brad and I come over for dinner tonight? I assume Mikey would want to join us, too. Invite Mack.

Laurel debated whether to mention Mack at all, but she figured she ought to bite the bullet. No good would come from excluding him. That would just cause unnecessary strain within the family.

Maureen replied right away.

Be here at 7. I'll make meatloaf.

Feeling accomplished, Laurel texted both Brad and Mikey with the arrangements. She felt a little bad for not inviting her other siblings, but thought she could do better convincing with a smaller crowd.

Lilly sighed mightily, as if she'd been working hard all day. She tucked her muzzle against Laurel's knee. The pair drifted into a cozy, peaceful slumber.

When she awoke, it was nearly dark outside. Checking the time on her phone, Laurel rolled over onto her back and stretched. As she did, she felt a tiny flutter in her lower abdomen. The sensation was faint, but it was there. It felt sort of like a butterfly moving around inside of her. When the realization hit her, she practically leaped off the couch with excitement. She'd read about this in the baby books. She was feeling her baby kick for the very first time.

Lilly startled at Laurel's sudden movements.

"It's our baby, Lilly! I felt our baby kick. Daddy is going to be so excited when he hears. Maybe he'll be able to feel it, too."

Laurel paused as she realized she'd just referred to Brad as daddy. Things were changing, and it felt right.

On cue, Brad's cruiser pulled into the driveway. Laurel practically bounced to the door to greet him. She wrapped her arms around his neck and kissed him passionately.

"Well, hello, my love," he said, taking her into his arms. "What has you so excited?"

Lilly bounced at Brad's side, insisting she be included, so he scooped her up and held her between them.

"I felt our baby kick!"

"Really?" Brad asked, a huge grin spreading across his features. "When?"

"Just before you pulled in," Laurel replied. "I'm not sure if you'll be able to feel it, but want to try?"

"Absolutely," he said.

Assuming she needed to by laying on her back to feel the sensation again, Laurel led him to the sofa. Then she stretched out and placed Brad's hand against her skin. Excitement turned to disappointment when he couldn't feel anything. Lilly wasn't sure what to make of the changing emotions.

"I guess it's too early," Laurel said. "I barely felt anything. It was like a butterfly fluttering."

"That's okay," Brad said. "It'll happen. I'm a patient man." He leaned over to kiss her again. "Actually, there's somewhere I want to take you. Are you ready to go?"

"We have dinner at Mom's at seven," she said. "Did you see my text?"

He nodded. "I did. We'll be done with this in plenty of time. Trust me. Lilly can tag along."

She agreed, then they both went to freshen up and change

clothes for the evening. Laurel made time to eat a granola bar, enough to hold her over until dinner. A short while later, they climbed into Brad's truck. He drove this time, and he made a fuss out of having to scoot the seat back after Laurel had been driving. It was all in good fun, though. He didn't actually mind. Lilly sat on Laurel's lap, an upgrade from her former position in the backseat.

While they rode, Brad filled her in on some progress that had been made in Baby Jasper's case.

"Hazel's guy has been arrested," he explained. "His name is Kevin Clark. His DNA was matched to samples found in your car. Once that evidence came back, he sang like a canary. We now have something to go on that will, hopefully, lead us to The Cradler. Jimmy and his team are all over it."

"That's amazing news. So, maybe we'll find the baby before the ransom deadline?"

"That's the hope. We'll see how it goes," Brad replied. "But enough of that talk, for now. I'm taking you somewhere special. Somewhere that's just about us."

"Okay," she said. "One more question and then I'll leave it alone. Is Kevin the one who grabbed me from the Christmas market? Kanesha's description of him made it sound like a different guy."

"No, Kevin claims he was responsible for getting rid of the car the next day. He didn't clean it well enough, though, because he left DNA behind. He does other miscellaneous tasks for The Cradler, including searching the computer in your dad's office. Jimmy's team is processing that, too. We should have more answers very soon."

"Good."

They pulled into the square downtown, where holiday

decorations twinkled brightly. Strings of white and colored lights were being strung along the main streets, and large red and gold bows adorned the lampposts. The air was crisp, scented with pine from the freshly placed wreaths and garlands. It was colder now that the sun had set. Brad kept a hand on his love, keeping her warm.

As he parked the truck and they exited, Brad led Laurel toward a beautifully lit part of the square. In front of the old, majestic fountain, a small ensemble of brass musicians was setting up— a trumpet, a French horn, and a trombone. Laurel's eyes widened as she recognized the French horn player, a colleague from a time that she subbed in the Nashville Symphony.

"Brad, what's going on?" Laurel asked, delight in her voice.

Brad smiled as they approached the musicians. "I thought we'd start this evening with a bit of music. And not just any music," he added as they stopped in front of the trio. The musicians nodded in greeting, then began to play a beautiful rendition of "L-O-V-E," a song that held special meaning for both of them—it was the piece Laurel had performed in a trio just like this one when Brad had first realized he was in love with her.

It had been after her Air Force Band days, but she'd played in the trio with a couple of friends for the sheer enjoyment of it. This particular performance had taken place on the National Mall in Washington, D.C., where the group was performing jazzy renditions of popular hits to get visitors in a happy mood. Laurel had told Brad that, since jazz wasn't her strength, the performance might not be very good. For his part, Brad had become enamored with Laurel and her many talents, vowing there and then to make her his wife someday.

"Aww," Laurel cooed. "The horn is taking the lead, just like I did."

"That's right," Brad replied. "Did you think I'd forget the details? I never could."

Lilly was leashed at their side, and she leaned her little head against Laurel's leg. It was a show of support. Lilly was a good dog.

The music filled the air, weaving around them as they stood hand in hand, immersed in the melody that seemed to narrate their own love story. Laurel felt transported back to D.C., and to a time when she and Brad first fell in love. Having the musical experience now, in her hometown of Appleman's Gap, was incredibly moving. Brad knew how to touch her heart.

A few onlookers had gathered, drawn by the beauty of the music. When the song ended, they burst into a soft round of applause.

Brad turned to Laurel, his eyes gleaming with emotion under the soft glow of the streetlights. "Laurel, my love, when I heard you play this song years ago, I knew there was something magical about you. Over the years, that magic has only grown, becoming a part of my everyday life, a part that I never want to lose." He reached into his coat pocket, pulling out a small velvet box, and got down on one knee, right there beside the fountain, under the twinkling lights.

"Oh, my God," Laurel said, taken aback by what was happening. She'd known this was coming, but she hadn't realized it would be so soon.

"Laurel, you've filled my life with love and joy. Will you marry me and make me the happiest man in the world?"

Tears welled up in Laurel's eyes, reflecting the twinkling lights. "Do you promise to always tell me the truth?"

"Of course."

"And to never keep anything from me?" she asked.

Brad sighed. "Babe, don't ask that. I promise to protect you and never, ever hurt you or do anything that would put you in harm's way. Can we leave it at that?"

Laurel hesitated, but she wanted this. She wanted a life with Brad, and their baby. She should have said yes when he'd proposed to her before. It was time to take a leap of faith. She nodded enthusiastically. "Yes, Brad! Yes, I will marry you!"

Brad slipped the ring onto her finger as it sparkled under the lights. He stood up and they embraced tightly, the musicians playing a soft rendition of "Isn't She Lovely." Brad whispered into her ear, "Every day with you is a dream come true, and I can't wait for our future together."

Laurel rested her head against Brad's chest, feeling the steady beat of his heart, her mind replaying the flutter of their baby inside her as if in tune with the night's harmony. "This is perfect, Brad. I couldn't have dreamed of a better proposal."

"You don't mind that it's the same ring?" he asked.

"I love that it's the same ring. You picked it out for me, and I will wear it proudly," she said with a smile.

As they pulled away from the embrace, Brad gave her a tender kiss, the kind that promised so much more. The brass trio wrapped up their set, and the couple thanked them warmly before heading back to the truck.

"Let's go share the good news," Brad said, his voice full of excitement as he held the door open for her. "Maureen ought to be happy about this."

"Everyone will be," Laurel replied. "You're already like a part of the family. We all love you."

"We can tell them about the baby, too."

Laurel nodded. "Yes, let's go tell everyone. Tonight is a celebration of so many things," she said, her voice brimming with happiness.

They drove off towards Maureen's house, the ring on Laurel's finger glinting under the streetlights. The winter air was cold outside, but inside Brad's truck, there was nothing but warmth and the promise of a future filled with love and family.

Twenty-Five

WITH LILLY IN TOW, Laurel and Brad arrived at Maureen's sprawling modern farmhouse. The warm glow from the windows promised a haven from the crisp evening air. Laurel was excited to share their good news with her mom, but given the contentious subject of paying Baby Jasper's ransom, she knew that the night ahead might be anything but peaceful.

As they entered, the rich aroma of meatloaf filled the air, mingling with the scent of freshly baked bread and something sweet, likely apple pie. Maureen, always the hostess, emerged from the kitchen, wiping her hands on her apron. Her smile was warm, but her eyes darted quickly to Mack, who sat awkwardly on the sofa, trying to appear at ease.

"Welcome, welcome!" Maureen exclaimed, coming over to hug Laurel and Brad as they hung their coats by the door. "Come on in and sit a spell. Dinner's almost ready. I have some trimmings for Lilly that I cooked up into a gravy."

"She'll love that." Laurel hugged her mom back, whispering quickly, "We need to talk about something important tonight, okay?"

"A few things, actually," Brad said.

Maureen nodded, a look of concern passing over her features before she turned to greet Mikey, who arrived downstairs, his expression serious.

"What'd I miss?" Mikey asked, hugging his sister then giving Brad a fist bump. Ryan had gone back to college in Murfreesboro, leaving Mikey as their mom's only houseguest. Other than Mack, that was.

Laurel couldn't contain her excitement. She flashed her engagement ring in Mikey's direction. He raised his brows and smiled happily. He didn't say anything, though, and Laurel shot him a look that let him know he should wait to discuss it out loud. Mikey nodded his understanding, his mood noticeably better than it was a moment before.

The family dinner table—the one at the back of the house—was set with Maureen's best china, an effort to make the occasion feel special despite the undercurrents of tension. They all took their seats, Mack last to join, settling next to Maureen with a cautious smile.

As they began to pass around dishes, Brad decided to break the ice. "Maureen, everything smells wonderful. You've outdone yourself."

"Oh, it's nothing," Maureen waved him off, but her cheeks pinked with pleasure. "I'm just glad to have you all here. I'm happy as a dead pig in the sunshine."

Everyone smiled, getting a kick out of Maureen's spunk and colorful Southern sayings. They were all used to it by now.

Dinner progressed with the usual small talk—updates

about work, the latest town gossip, and gentle teasing between siblings. Laurel decided to begin with the good news. She clasped Brad's hand, ready to hold his hand in the air with hers as she showed off her engagement ring.

"Well, dear," Maureen said to her daughter. "We're off like a herd of turtles. Did you have something to tell me?"

Laurel nodded, a toothy grin covering her face. "Mom, Mikey ... Mack, Brad and I are engaged!"

She held up her new engagement ring to show. Maureen put one hand over her mouth, an expression of happy shock taking over.

"It's about time, you two," Maureen said.

"Congratulations, Sis," Mikey added, then "Welcome to the family, Brad. I've been rooting for you."

"That he has," Laurel confirmed.

"Congratulations," Mack said simply.

Laurel and Brad thanked everyone.

Brad looked at her playfully. "Should we tell them the rest?"

Laurel grinned from ear to ear, letting her hand rest on her lower abdomen. "I'm pregnant. We're having a baby!"

Maureen smiled knowingly. She'd guessed that secret days ago, even though they hadn't had a chance to talk about it. Mikey knew, of course. And Mack was too far removed to have a big reaction. Still, the group cheered and congratulated the parents-to-be.

"Does this mean you're moving back to Appleman's Gap, Laurel?" Maureen asked. "You're grinning like a possum eating a sweet tater. I hope that means your answer is yes."

Laurel and Brad hadn't discussed that part yet. Laurel wanted to say yes to moving back. She knew she should say yes. Brad had an important job here as Police Chief, and he was good at it. Her dad would be proud. But she wasn't quite ready. "I'm not completely sure," she said, glancing at Brad. "Our lives have been in D.C. for so long."

Brad sighed, but he leaned in and gave Laurel a reassuring squeeze. "We have plenty of time to figure all of that out. As long as we're together, that's where I want to be."

Lilly woofed her agreement, which made everyone chuckle.

"Well, whatever you decide will be just fine," Maureen said. "I'm happy for the both of you."

They thanked Maureen, then the mood shifted. The elephant in the room couldn't be ignored for long. As they began to clear the dishes, Laurel caught her mother's eye, signaling it was time for a more serious discussion.

Gathering in the living room, Brad took the lead, his voice gentle yet firm. "Maureen, we need to talk about the situation with Baby Jasper."

Maureen's face tightened. "Yes, I suppose we do."

Laurel took a deep breath, feeling Brad's supportive hand on her back. "Mom, the F.B.I. is waiting to hear if you'll cooperate with the ransom demand. It's a lot of money, but it might be the only way to ensure the baby's safety."

Maureen shook her head, her hands clasped tightly in her lap. "That's an impossible amount. How could they expect us to come up with that?"

Mikey leaned forward, his tone earnest. "We're not saying it's easy, Mom. But maybe, with the resources from Dad's investments ... then it could be coming from him, sort of. You know?"

The mention of Cornelius caused a sharp intake of breath

from Maureen, her eyes flickering to Mack, who had remained silent. Mack's presence, so soon after Cornelius' supposed death, was a complication none of them wanted to delve into deeply—not yet.

"It's complicated," Maureen murmured, looking down. Mack put a hand on her shoulder, a silent offer of support that didn't go unnoticed.

Brad continued, "We're exploring every option, Maureen. Negotiating, looking for assets. Anything to bring him back safely."

The room fell silent, each lost in their thoughts, the weight of the decision pressing down on them. Lilly, sensing the tension, whined softly, nuzzling against Laurel's leg.

Laurel looked at her mother, her voice soft but determined. "Mom, think about what Dad would have wanted. He'd have moved heaven and earth to bring Jasper back."

At the mention of Cornelius, a look of anger crossed Maureen's face. She had clearly been hurt by her husband, and she wouldn't get over that easily.

"Lower than a snake's belly in a wagon rut," she muttered. "I'm not sure I care what he would have wanted."

Once again, Laurel marveled at how quickly her mom's attitude had changed. A few days ago, Maureen was crying because she missed her longtime love. Was there something her mother wasn't saying?

As they concluded the conversation with no firm decision, the night grew deeper, and the shadows outside lengthened. Laurel and Brad exchanged a look, a silent agreement that they were far from done with this discussion. The weight of the evening's discourse was heavy on their hearts.

Maureen's eyes wandered to Mack, seeking some form of

reassurance or guidance, but Mack seemed lost in his own thoughts. His silence was unusual, adding another layer of tension to an already strained atmosphere.

Mack finally spoke, his voice low and cautious. "Maureen, I know this is hard. But maybe it's not just about what Cornelius would have wanted. It's about what's right for Jasper now. We have to consider all our options, even the difficult ones. Like I told you, I can pay the ransom. Some or all of it. Whatever you need. If The Cradler insists it come from you, well then I can pay you directly to replenish your reserves."

Maureen nodded slowly, her expression softening slightly. "You're right, Mack. It's just ... hard to think about bailing Cornelius out, knowing everything now."

Laurel sensed the unspoken words hanging in the air, the secrets that seemed to be on the tip of her mother's tongue. She decided to gently push a little further, hoping to uncover more about her father's mysterious actions and their current predicament. "Mom, is there something about Dad you haven't told us? Something that might help us understand all of this better?"

Maureen sighed, a weary sound that seemed to carry the weight of many unshared burdens. "It's not the right time, Laurel. But soon, I'll need to tell you and the other kids everything. For now, let's focus on Jasper and getting him home safely."

Brad, sensing the emotional toll the conversation was taking on Laurel, decided to lighten the mood. "Well, let's not forget some good news amidst all this," he chimed in, wrapping an arm around Laurel. "We're getting married, and soon there'll be a new addition to the family."

This brought a smile to everyone's faces, even Maureen's, who managed a chuckle and shook her head. "Yes, and I'm thrilled about that. Really, I am. It's a blessing."

As they wrapped up the evening, promises were made to revisit the conversation about the ransom and explore all possible avenues for funding it.

Mikey, who had been quiet for most of the discussion, finally added, "We'll figure this out, Mom. We'll do it together."

They all agreed to meet again the next day, with Brad promising to pull in some favors from his contacts in law enforcement to see if any more progress had been made on finding the kidnappers. If they were lucky, they'd find them and rescue Baby Jasper before Maureen had to pay the ransom.

As Laurel and Brad prepared to leave, Laurel pulled her mother into a tight hug. "We'll get through this, Mom. We always do."

Maureen held her daughter close, then whispered, "I know, dear. Thank you. And Laurel, about your father ... be prepared. There's more to his story than you know."

The drive home was quiet, with both Laurel and Brad lost in their thoughts. The night's revelations and the hints at deeper secrets had stirred a mix of emotions in Laurel—from hope for her future with Brad and their baby, to uncertainty about her father's mysterious past and the shadow it cast over their family.

As they arrived home, Brad squeezed Laurel's hand reassuringly. "No matter what comes, we're in this together. All the way."

Laurel nodded, feeling the comfort of his presence.

"Maybe we should forget about the stress and drama for another night. Like you told me, we can worry about all of that tomorrow."

"I like the sound of that. What should we do instead?"

Laurel pushed Brad onto the sofa, then climbed onto his lap, kissing him seductively. "I'd say a celebration is in order."

"Oh, is that right, future Mrs. Tate?"

Laurel swatted at him playfully. "Hey, now, I never said I was changing my last name. One step at a time."

"Yeah, yeah," he replied between kisses. "Call yourself anything you want. As long as I can call you my wife."

Lilly settled into her bed on the floor as Laurel and Brad moved to the bedroom. They had much to celebrate, and celebrate, they did. It was a night to remember.

Outside, under the glow of the streetlights, the faintest impression of a figure watching from the shadows could have been dismissed as a trick of the light. But for those who believed, it was a sign that Cornelius, though hidden from sight, was not far from the heart of this ordeal, his presence still watching over them, his secrets buried like embers waiting to ignite.

Twenty-Six

THE MORNING after their intense family dinner at Maureen's house, the town of Appleman's Gap was abuzz with more than its usual small-town gossip.

At Leopold's Diner, where Laurel and Mikey planned to meet again, the atmosphere was charged with concern and curiosity. The Nashville news had picked up on the story of Baby Jasper's kidnapping, and with it, the hefty ransom demand Maureen was facing. The story had also mentioned Mack Roberts, making the entire ordeal sound as dramatic as a soap opera.

Before Laurel arrived, Sarah had made a tearful plea on television, begging Maureen to cooperate with the kidnappers. "Please, we just want our baby boy home safely. He needs his family ... and we need him."

Fortunately, Sarah hadn't mentioned the fact that she was Cornelius' illegitimate daughter. The reporters knew, though, and they had explained the connection in detail. Their tone was condescending. Laurel didn't like it one bit. She hated that her family had become the talk of the town, in Appleman's Gap and beyond.

Outside the diner, the sentiment was a mix of sympathy and frustration. Tyrese Wilson, a long-time local and frequent visitor to Dane Family Orchards, was overheard loudly criticizing Maureen's hesitation. "She's got the means. If she doesn't pay up to bring that baby back, I say we boycott the orchard. We can't support a family business that won't help one of their own!"

He had a point.

Inside, Laurel caught snippets of these conversations as she slid into the booth across from Mikey. The weight of public opinion was yet another layer of pressure, but her focus shifted when she saw the grave look on her brother's face.

"What's up, Mikey? You look like you've seen a ghost," Laurel said, her voice thick with worry.

Mikey tried to deflect. "Who do you think tipped the news station off?"

"I don't know," she replied. "Someone with access to the information. Maybe someone in the police department? My guess would be Detective Josh Nolan. He seemed to have it out for me, for some reason. I'm not sure what I ever did to him. Maybe he had a beef with Dad. I'm not sure if he worked in Appleman's Gap when Dad was Chief. But enough of that. Tell me what's wrong."

Mikey hesitated, but finally leaned in, lowering his voice. "Look, I've been digging around, trying to find anything that could help with Dad's old cases or any of his hidden files."

Laurel's eyes widened, both alarmed and intrigued. "I

guess that's better than hacking the F.B.I. Did you find something?"

"I found encrypted files on an old hard drive in Dad's study. They're heavily secured, but from what I can tell, they might be connected to some major criminal networks. I haven't cracked them yet, but I think Dad was onto something big. Maybe even linked to what's happening now."

"That's huge, Mikey. We need to get into those files," Laurel whispered, the possibilities spinning in her head. "Want me to call Jimmy so that his team can work on it."

"Not yet," Mikey said. "Give me some time first."

Before Laurel could say more, her phone rang. It was Kanesha.

"Hey!" Laurel said cheerfully. They'd known she'd come up with something else. Kanesha had a knack for noticing things others overlooked.

"Hey, Laurel, I found something odd at Jack and Jill's this morning. Can I come by and show you?"

"Absolutely. We're at Leopold's Diner for our morning meeting," Laurel responded, curious about what Kanesha might have discovered. "We haven't even ordered our food yet. You're welcome to join us."

"Good. Order me a coffee."

A short time later, Kanesha slid into the booth beside Mikey, her expression serious. "I was cleaning up this morning before we opened when I found this under one of the tables."

She handed Laurel a crumpled piece of paper. It was a hastily written note that mentioned a meeting place and time, with the initials K.C.

"Kevin Clark," Laurel said, glancing at Mikey.

"Who's that?" Kanesha asked.

Mikey and Laurel exchanged a look, realizing the significance of what Kanesha had found. "This could be a lead to where they were planning something or maybe even where they're holding Jasper," Mikey murmured, examining the note further.

"Kevin Clark is the guy you saw with Hazel at the apple barn. He was arrested yesterday. His DNA was found in my stolen car," Laurel explained. "Good work, Kanesha."

Kanesha's eyes lit up. "Maybe the person who dropped this note was supposed to meet him, before he got arrested."

"Maybe."

As they discussed their findings, Laurel remembered they were expected at her mother's house for dinner again that evening. "We need to keep digging into Dad's files and follow up on this note. Tonight at Mom's, we can update everyone and plan our next steps."

Kanesha nodded, her eyes bright with the thrill of the hunt. "I'll keep my ears open at work today. You never know what else might turn up."

"Please do," Mikey said. "Call us if you have anything at all. You're welcome to join us for dinner."

Kanesha smiled bashfully. It was obvious that she had taken a shine to Mikey. If he weren't married, she'd be hitting on him. No doubt. The feeling seemed to be mutual, but there was mutual respect there, too. Neither would cross the line.

"You're sweet," Kanesha said, "but I'm not coming to your momma's house."

"Suit yourself," Mikey replied.

Kanesha downed her coffee, then they said their goodbyes. She had to get back to work at Jack and Jill's before the lunch rush.

Laurel and Mikey ordered breakfast, more oatmeal and another omelet, a repeat of the day before. Ginger was their waitress again, too. The scene felt familiar. Comforting. Mikey had visibly relaxed.

"Kanesha is fond of you," Laurel said with a smile.

"Stop it," Mikey said. "You know Jess has my heart. But there's no denying that Kanesha is a beautiful, intelligent woman. Maybe I'll set her up with one of my friends."

They laughed, the mood lightening further. It was finally beginning to feel like they were making progress. Maybe they would bring Baby Jasper home safe, after all. Laurel sent out quick texts to both Jimmy and Brad, letting them know the initials and address that Kanesha had found.

As they waited for their food, Mikey's expression turned serious again, and he leaned forward, his voice dropping to a whisper. "Sis, I've been meaning to ask you about something you said yesterday. You mentioned being scared it would happen again. What did you mean by that?"

Laurel sighed, her gaze dropping to the table before meeting her brother's concerned eyes. "I've been having a hard time these past days, Mikey. After what happened at the holiday market, when I was thrown in the trunk and taken with Baby Jasper. It's stirred a lot up."

Mikey reached across the table, offering a supportive hand. "You're an F.B.I. agent, Laurel. You handle danger all the time."

"Yeah."

"But this is different, isn't it?" he asked.

"It is," Laurel admitted, her voice barely above a whisper.

"I think I'm scared of being kidnapped again. It's irrational, I know. I shouldn't feel this way, given my training, but it's there. This fear."

Mikey's expression softened. "It's not irrational, Laurel. It's human. Especially since Dad was investigating a kidnapping syndicate before he died. Could there be a connection?"

Laurel paused, the mention of her Dad's investigation sparking a flicker of something deep within her—a memory long repressed. "I sometimes think I remember something, but the memories are just out of reach. Like shadows in the fog. I don't know if they're real or just something I've constructed."

"Maybe it's worth exploring," Mikey suggested gently. "Not just for the case, but for you. To heal."

"Maybe so."

Laurel nodded slowly, considering his words. Their food arrived, breaking the moment, but the conversation had shifted something in Laurel.

As they ate, they made small talk, chatting about the media circus and whether or not their mom was going to pay the ransom. They agreed to dig deeper into their father's encrypted files after dinner that night, hopeful that it might shed light on both the kidnapping syndicate and perhaps even Cornelius' involvement.

"You know," Mikey said between bites of cheesy omelet, "I've been thinking about Mom and Mack Roberts."

Laurel nodded, understanding immediately. "It's weird, isn't it? Seeing her with someone else. I mean, Dad's only been gone—"

"Not long enough for it not to feel strange," Mikey

finished for her. "I'm trying to be supportive, but it's strange."

"Yeah, exactly," Laurel sighed, tucking a strand of hair behind her ear. "And Mack of all people. I never would've pictured those two together. You remember what Dad used to say about him?"

Mikey chuckled dryly. "That he wouldn't trust Mack Roberts to water his plants, let alone with anything important." He shook his head. "And now, here he is, having dinner at our family table."

"I don't know how well Dad actually knew him. I think he just knew him in high school, and he knew that Mack and Mom had stayed in touch as friends. But it feels like a betrayal, doesn't it?" Laurel's voice was low, her eyes not meeting Mikey's. "I mean, I want Mom to be happy, but it's like we're in some twisted reality."

Mikey looked at Laurel, his expression softening. "I know. It's hard seeing her move on, especially with him. But we've got bigger issues with Dad's files and this kidnapping case. Maybe Mack can be of some use if he's closer to Mom now. Did Brad have lunch with him yesterday?"

Laurel considered this, her brow furrowing. "Maybe. Yeah, Brad took him to lunch and asked him to help convince Mom to pay the ransom. He said it went okay. But still, I wonder if we're missing something about why he's really here."

Unbeknownst to Laurel, the pieces to this puzzle would soon collide in an unexpected way.

"Agreed," Mikey said as he cleaned the last bite from his plate.

When they were both finished eating, Laurel stayed to

visit the bathroom again as Mikey prepared to head back to Maureen's house and get busy decrypting their father's files.

"Take care of yourself, big sister," Mikey said.

"You, too, little brother. Thanks for sticking around Appleman's Gap and helping me sort all of this out. I don't know what I'd do without you."

They parted with a hug.

Twenty-Seven

AS SHE EXITED THE DINER, Laurel was barely aware of the chill biting through her coat, her mind racing with the details of Baby Jasper's case. The crisp air seemed to echo with the murmur of secrets just on the verge of being uncovered, each step taking her closer to truths that might change everything.

She reached for the door of Brad's truck, her hand shaking slightly—not from the cold, but from the adrenaline that had sustained her throughout the recent days. The stress was beginning to catch up to her. She had tried to pretend like she was okay, but that would only last so long. Perhaps another afternoon nap with Lilly was in order. The dog had a way of soothing Laurel and calming her nerves. Being calm was good for the baby.

Something kept bothering Laurel, though. A memory at the edges of her consciousness seemed to want to make itself known. The details were fuzzy, but something was there. Something that terrified her.

As Laurel fumbled with her keys, a sudden sharp noise behind her made her spin around. Before she could register what was happening, a heavy cloth bag was thrown over her head, muffling her screams and plunging her into darkness. Her last fleeting thought before succumbing to the chloroformed interior of the bag was a prayer that someone had noticed her abduction. This time, there wouldn't be an extra phone at her disposal.

When Laurel awoke, she found herself in a dimly lit, musty room. Her wrists were tied behind her back, her ankles bound tightly together. The memories of her previous kidnapping from the holiday market surged forward, but this time, something else pushed through the haze of her fear—flickers of another time, another fear, from when she was just a child. Memories she had buried deep, of being taken, of crying out for her father, of a dark room much like this one. The realization that she had experienced this terror before as a child left her reeling.

Could her childhood experience be why she found herself pursuing a career with the Bureau? Would she have gone into a different line of work, had it never happened? A professional horn player was unlikely to find themselves in the kind of danger Laurel was in now.

"What's happening?" she tried to ask. Her speech came out muffled.

Her heart hammered in her chest as she fought to calm her breathing, to think despite the panic. She needed to escape, but more than that, she needed to understand. Why her? Why again? She'd thought the kidnapping at the holiday market was about Baby Jasper. That they'd wanted to hold him for ransom. Why had they released her then but taken her now? The questions circled in her mind like vultures.

Hours seemed to pass with only the sound of her own shallow breaths for company. She thought about Brad and how sick with worry he'd be when she didn't arrive home. She thought about Mikey and how guilty he'd feel to know that he could have helped her if he'd waited at the diner just five more minutes. She also thought about her mom, who would hate herself for being so preoccupied with Mack Roberts that she'd failed to protect her own daughter and grandchild.

Maybe that last part wasn't fair.

Then, footsteps approached, a key turned in the lock, and the door creaked open. A silhouette appeared—a man, broad-shouldered and imposing.

"You remember, don't you?" the figure spoke, his voice chillingly familiar.

Laurel squinted, trying to make out his features in the dim light. "Who are you? What do you want from me?" she demanded, her voice hoarse. "My mom's not going to pay any more ransom, if that's what you think. I'm not sure she has it."

The man stepped forward, into the light, and all the blood drained from Laurel's face. She couldn't believe what she was seeing. She shook her head in an attempt to shake free of this. To bring herself back to a reality that made sense.

It was impossible, yet there he stood. Cornelius Dane, her father, who she had mourned, who she had believed dead for months.

"Dad?" she whispered, disbelief coloring her tone. "You're alive?"

Cornelius knelt before her, cutting her bonds with a swift motion. "I had to make them believe I was gone, Laurel. It was the only way to keep you safe while I investigated The Cradler. They're not just kidnappers. They're a dangerous syndicate, and they have their claws in too many to risk exposing myself."

Laurel rubbed her wrists, the reality of her father's words sinking in. "You let us believe you were dead. Mom, Mikey, all of us. For what? How could you? Do you have any idea how scared I was being taken from Leopold's parking lot? And the chloroform? That stuff is dangerous."

She thought about how bad it was for the baby to be exposed. She wasn't sure about the effects of chloroform on a fetus in the second trimester. She prayed the exposure wouldn't cause permanent harm. How terrible it would be if her own father caused her unborn baby to have birth defects, or worse. Hadn't he created enough trouble for the family?

Laurel was so mad, she wanted to punch her dad, square in the nose. At the same time, though, she loved him dearly. Even if he had cheated on her mom. He had always been a good father to her. They'd been close. Seeing him again was a dream come true. How could she feel anything but gratitude?

"Faking my death was the hardest decision of my life," Cornelius said, his eyes filled with torment. "But I uncovered things, Laurel. This goes deeper than we ever imagined. Your abduction as a child, the recent case—they're connected. The Cradler and his goons have been orchestrating this for decades. And his father did it before him, although The Cradler seems far worse than his father ever was." He paused, looking regretful. "I'm sorry about the chloroform. I wasn't sure what else to do."

She shook her head, then reached forward to embrace her dad. Even if she was mad at him, she was grateful that he was alive. They hugged tightly, for a long while. In her dad's arms, Laurel remembered leaning her head on his shoulder as a child. The safety she'd always felt when he was around. She hadn't been ready to lose him.

"I love you, Dad," she said softly. Then, "I was kidnapped as a kid?"

He nodded. "I love you, too, Laurel. Yes, you were kidnapped when you were three years-old. Your mother was beside herself with worry. We got you back, but I'm not sure Maureen ever forgave me. She believed that my connection with law enforcement made you a target. Truthfully, she was probably right."

"I don't remember," Laurel said. "Well, just barely. There are memories that seem to want to surface."

"That makes sense. You were young, and the experience was traumatic. We aren't sure what happened to you during that time."

Laurel put a hand against her lower abdomen, instinctively protective of her own baby. "I can't imagine."

She had a lot to tell her dad, but there would be time to catch up later. They had more pressing matters at hand.

From another room, Laurel heard a baby fuss. It was mild, like the baby knew he or she was safe and would be tended to.

"Is that ...?" Laurel asked.

Cornelius smiled, proud of his handiwork. He stepped into the next room and could be heard talking gently to the baby. When he stepped out with the infant in his arms, it was Baby Jasper, safe and sound. Jasper's big brown eyes were moist with tears, but he leaned his head against Cornelius' shoulder. He was okay.

"Here he is," Cornelius said.

"All along, we had help behind the scenes," Laurel mused. "Jimmy and Brad will be so relieved."

"They know."

That took Laurel by surprise. "They what?"

"I mean, they just learned that Jasper was safe in my care when I called them a few minutes ago. They were working the case to bring him home just as diligently as I was," he explained.

"So, they knew you were alive?" Laurel asked, her emotions hot and cold as she considered the ramifications. She'd known the two of them were hiding something.

Cornelius nodded. "They did. Don't be too upset with them. I didn't give them much choice. Revealing that my death was faked would have compromised the investigation. It still could. You can't tell anyone, Laurel. Not even Mikey."

"You don't understand, Dad," she said. "Mikey has been helping me with this. He's one of my closest friends, in addition to being my brother. I can't keep him in the dark. He'll keep your secret, I promise." That reminded her. "Do you know what's happening with Mom?"

Laurel wasn't sure whether she should mention Mack, but she felt like she needed to say something.

Cornelius pursed his lips as he bounced Jasper in his arms. "Yeah, I heard that everyone knows about Sarah and that Jasper here is my grandson. Your mom knew all along, but she didn't want other people finding out. This must have been a hard week for her. For what it's worth, I'm sorry. I never meant to hurt any of you."

"That might be too little too late," Laurel said. "I don't know. Mom is dating Mack Roberts. He arrived from Colorado the other day."

Cornelius dropped his head. Apparently, he didn't know that part. "I made contact with her the other day. Bringing Mack into the picture must have been a reaction to learning that I'm still alive. I can't say that I blame her, but I don't want to lose her. I love that sassy woman with all of my heart."

Laurel shrugged. "Maybe it will just take time. I'm not sure. How about we get Jasper home to his family now? We can deal with the rest later."

"Jimmy is already on his way. Jasper will be in his mother's arms within the hour."

"Good," Laurel said, reaching out and stroking the boy's —her nephew's—chubby cheek.

The weight of her father's investigation, of his sacrifice, pressed down on her. Laurel felt the world tilt, her professional instincts kicking in. She'd known that he'd been investigating a crime syndicate before he died, and that he'd gone undercover to do it. She hadn't known that she'd been taken as a child or that her dad was so determined to bring these people to justice. Naturally, she wanted to help.

"We need to bring them down, Dad. Tell me what you need me to do."

Cornelius nodded. "That's why I had you brought here. I need your help, Laurel. You're the key to blowing this whole operation wide open."

TO BE CONTINUED.

. . .

Get Book 2 in the series, *Ties That Bind Her.*

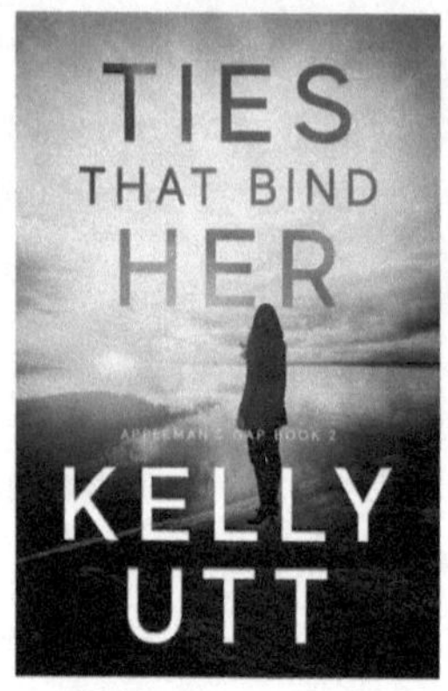

Enjoy this book?

A NOTE FROM AUTHOR KELLY UTT

Did you enjoy this book? You can make a big difference.

Honest reviews of my books help bring them to the attention of other readers.

If you've enjoyed this book, I would be very grateful if you could spend just five minutes leaving a review (it can be as short as you like) on the book's retail page where you purchased and on Goodreads or BookBub.

Thank you very much.

STANDARDS OF STARLIGHT BOOKS
KELLY UTT

Kelly Utt writes emotional, pulse-pounding suspense, family saga, and women's fiction novels. The stakes are high. The twists and turns will keep you on the edge of your seat.

Kelly was raised by a dad who would read a book, ask her to read it, too, and then insist they discuss it together, igniting her passion for life's big questions. That passion is often reflected in her novels, giving them a depth which leaves readers wanting more and thinking about her stories long after the last lines are read.

Kelly holds a Bachelor's degree in psychology from the University of Tennessee, Knoxville and she studied graduate-level interactive media and communications at Quinnipiac University.

She lives in Nashville, Tennessee with her husband and sons. She also writes supernatural thrillers with one of her sons as the combined pen name Christopher Kelly.

www.kellyutt.com